DEKOK AND THE DANCING DEATH

"DeKok" Books by A.C. Baantjer:

Published in the United States:
- Murder in Amsterdam
- DeKok and the Sunday Strangler
- DeKok and the Corpse on Christmas Eve
- DeKok and the Somber Nude
- DeKok and the Dead Harlequin
- DeKok and the Sorrowing Tomcat
- DeKok and the Disillusioned Corpse
- DeKok and the Careful Killer
- DeKok and the Romantic Murder
- DeKok and the Dying Stroller
- DeKok and the Corpse at the Church Wall
- DeKok and the Dancing Death
- DeKok and Murder on the Menu

Available soon from InterContinental Publishing:
- DeKok and the Naked Lady
- DeKok and the Brothers of the Easy Death
- DeKok and the Deadly Accord
- DeKok and Murder in Seance
- DeKok and Murder in Ecstasy
- DeKok and the Begging Death
- DeKok and the Geese of Death
- DeKok and Murder by Melody
- DeKok and Death of a Clown
- DeKok and Variations on Murder
- DeKok and Murder by Installments
- DeKok and Murder on Blood Mountain
- DeKok and the Dead Lovers
- DeKok and the Mask of Death
- DeKok and the Corpse by Return
- DeKok and Murder in Bronze
- DeKok and the Deadly Warning
- DeKok and Murder First Class
- DeKok and the Vendetta
- DeKok and Murder Depicted
- DeKok and Dance Macabre
- DeKok and the Disfiguring Death
- DeKok and the Devil's Conspiracy
- DeKok and the Duel at Night
- and more ...

DeKok and the Dancing Death

by
BAANTJER

translated from the Dutch by H.G. Smittenaar

INTERCONTINENTAL PUBLISHING

ISBN 1 881164 11 X

DEKOK AND THE DANCING DEATH. English translation copyright © 1994 by InterContinental Publishing. Translated from *De Cock en de dansende dood*, by Baantjer [Albert Cornelis Baantjer], copyright © 1978 by Uitgeverij De Fontein, Baarn, Netherlands. All rights reserved. Printed in the United States of America. No part of this book may be used or reproduced in any manner whatsoever without written permission except in the case of brief quotations embodied in critical articles or reviews. For information address InterContinental Publishing, Box 7242, Fairfax Station, Virginia, 22039.

Printing History:
    1st Dutch printing: 1978
    2nd Dutch printing: 1979
    3rd Dutch printing: 1980
    4th Dutch printing: 1982
    5th Dutch printing: 1985
    6th Dutch printing: 1987
    7th Dutch printing: 1987
    8th Dutch printing: 1988
    9th Dutch printing: 1988
    10th Dutch printing: 1988
    11th Dutch printing: 1989
    12th Dutch printing: 1990
    13th Dutch printing: 1991
    14th Dutch printing: 1992
    15th Dutch printing: 1993
    16th Dutch printing: 1993

    1st American edition: 1994

Typography: Monica S. Rozier
Cover Photo: Peter Coene

*DeKok
and the
Dancing Death*

1

It was a sultry summer evening in Amsterdam. The heat of the day still clung to the facades of the old houses in the inner city and shimmered above the canals and the cobblestones. An endless stream of tourists, surrounded by a cloud of strange languages and accents, walked along the wide pavement of the Damrak, the major street leading toward the Dam, the large, central square in the center of Amsterdam. Pigeons panted in the niches of the Royal Palace, built in 1648 and often called "the eighth wonder of the world". Nobody understood how the Dutch had managed to build such an imposing edifice on the soft, wet ground of the Netherlands. The secret consists of 13,659 wooden poles, the size of tree trunks, that were driven into the ground, one by one, to form the foundation of the building.

Younger tourists and part of the horde of foreign students that descend on the Netherlands every year, filled the steps of the War Memorial built to commemorate the heroism of Dutch *citizens* during the German occupation of the Second World War.

A young man strummed a guitar and a young woman danced barefoot to the sound of the music. The two formed a colorful complement to the busy but peaceful atmosphere on the large square.

Detective-Inspector DeKok of the old, renowned police station in Warmoes Street, paused and observed the tableau. The dancing girl fascinated him. She wore a white blouse, open to the waist, the swell of the full breasts clearly visible and her nipples strained against the thin material of the flimsy garment. A multicolored skirt, reaching almost to her ankles, completed her ensemble. Happily his eyes followed the supple movements of the slender body and he hoped fervently that her dance was indeed an expression of joy and not the result of drugs.

The gray detective suppressed the thought with an effort. I'll never learn, he thought, I should be enjoying the enchanting sight of a happy young woman and instead I think about drugs. I've been a cop too long. He shook his head and returned his full attention to the dancing girl. She continued to fascinate him and he watched as if hypnotized. The girl seemed oblivious to her surroundings and danced trance-like, swirling her skirt, moving her arms in graceful gestures and from time to time revealing long, shapely legs. DeKok worried that she might hurt her bare feet on the hard, sometimes sharp, cobblestones.

Almost imperceptibly, her movements became slower and she slid gracefully to the steps of the monument. She panted a little and was beaded with perspiration. She took a tambourine from a rucksack and tapped it rhythmically against her elbow, a perfect accompaniment to the soft strumming of the guitar. Suddenly she seemed to realize that she was being observed. She swung her long hair away from her face with a toss of her head and looked up. Her eyes met those of DeKok. She rested the tambourine in her lap and stared boldly at him, almost challenging. The gray sleuth withstood her eyes for several long moments and then, smiling, he walked on.

After about a hundred yards he turned around and looked back. He watched as she hoisted the rucksack on her back and walked in his direction. DeKok slowly ambled on, hoping she would overtake him. He wouldn't mind taking another, closer look at her. Halfway to the Mint, the forerunner of the New York Stock Exchange, he turned once more. She seemed to have closed the distance between them, but also seemed to adapt her speed to his own leisurely progress. DeKok shrugged his shoulders, scolded himself for a sentimental old fool and turned into Old Bridge Alley toward Warmoes Street, the oldest street in Amsterdam and home of the busiest police station in Europe. He waved cheerfully at a fat barkeeper who had just taken the shutters off his windows and stole a glance at a young prostitute, arm-in-arm with her pimp. With a part of his mind he placed the pimp and realized he had never seen the girl before.

The dancing girl had just about gone from his thoughts as he climbed the few bluestone steps toward the entrance of the station house. Inside, in the corridor, he suddenly heard the sound of heavy breathing.

"Mister DeKok?"

He turned around. He recognized her silhouette against the light from the street, the long hair, the slender figure, the bulge of the rucksack.

"You *are* . . . Mr. DeKok?"

The gray sleuth pushed his ever-present, decrepit little felt hat further back on his head and nodded.

". . . with kay-oh-kay," he agreed automatically.

She came a step closer. A tired smile fled across her face.

"Sorry . . . I followed you. I didn't quite dare speak to you in the street. You see, I didn't want the others . . ." She hesitated, did not complete the sentence. "Do you have some time for me?"

DeKok executed a stiff, old-fashioned bow. Without another word he led her toward the stairs leading to the detective room on the next floor. At the bottom of the stairs he helped take off her heavy rucksack, lifted it by one of the straps and carried it up the stairs. She followed demurely.

Vledder, DeKok's young assistant, partner and friend, was seated behind his desk, next to DeKok's desk, at the far end of the large detective room. Inevitably the young Inspector was busy on the keyboard of his computer terminal. When he became aware of DeKok's approach, he hit a sequence of keys, looked up and glanced at the clock.

"You took a long time."

DeKok gestured toward the girl.

"She detained me," he smiled.

He saw her for the first time close-up. In the harsh glare of the overhead lights he discovered she had blue eyes and full, pale pink lips. He placed the heavy rucksack on the floor and gave her a closer look. He estimated her to be in her early twenties, but the tanned face made it difficult to be precise. He pushed the rucksack aside and held a chair for her.

She hesitated, gave Vledder a hasty, hunted look. DeKok repeated his invitation and waved carelessly in Vledder's direction.

"Don't worry about him," he said in a friendly, soothing voice, "I've no secrets from Vledder. He's completely trustworthy." He gave her a winning smile. "Believe me, if necessary he'll be as silent as a grave."

Still barefoot, she came closer and seated herself on the edge of the chair he held for her. He walked around the desk and seated himself. She leaned closer to him.

"A grave," she whispered, "that's what it's all about."

DeKok's eyebrows rippled with a movement that did not seem possible. Many people were convinced that DeKok's eyebrows lived a life of their own and moved totally independent of DeKok's will and knowledge. Whatever the truth of the matter, it was a fact that DeKok's eyebrows could move in way that seemed more appropriate to the antennae of an insect than a detail of human anatomy.

The girl seemed momentarily stunned as she watched DeKok's forehead. It was not an unusual reaction from observers of the phenomenon. Vledder watched intently, he knew what would happen and he was right. As the display ended, the girl shook her head as if clearing her vision. She glanced quickly at Vledder and then back at DeKok. Then she decided, as Vledder knew she would, that she could not possibly have seen what she thought she saw and with visible effort she concentrated on DeKok's question.

"A grave?" he asked.

"Yes," she nodded slowly, ". . . yes, a grave for Colette. She can't stay that way."

DeKok cocked his head at her.

"And who is Colette?"

"A girl from Utrecht, I think," she answered, gesturing vaguely. "We've been together for a few months, now."

DeKok watched her intently, searchingly. He wondered if she was joking, or on drugs. Perhaps she suffered from hallucinations?

"And what's the matter with Colette?"

She looked at him. Her blue eyes were vacant, expressionless.

"She's dead," she said hoarsely. "She's been dead for two days."

Vledder swallowed and DeKok, too, thought it was hard to believe.

"Dead?" he asked after a considerable pause.

"Yes."

DeKok scratched the back of his neck.

"And you were dancing . . ." There was reproach in his voice.

She avoided his eyes, lowered her head.

"I always dance . . . when I'm troubled."

* * *

They left the old police station and at the end of Warmoes Street they penetrated deeper into the Red Light District. Vledder walked up front and DeKok followed, the girl on his arm. Some passers-by gave the couple a second look: the old, gray man with the young, striking, barefoot girl. DeKok was oblivious to the stares. The regular denizens of the Quarter smiled at him, or waved. DeKok greeted them with a nod, or a smile, in return. The crowds of tourists gaping at the girls in the windows, entering and leaving sex-shops and theaters and marveling at the free and easy atmosphere, might not know the gray sleuth, but he was a well-known figure in the neighborhood. It was curious that after many years, they still ignored Vledder. Vledder was a cop, they felt. But DeKok ... DeKok was simply DeKok. The Quarter would seem incomplete without him.

The special sounds of the Quarter engulfed them: a hundred languages, mixed with the raucous noise of several bars, the high-pitched voices of whores and the ceaseless calling of street vendors. It was a carnival atmosphere that could not be duplicated in any other city of the world. It was Amsterdam.

DeKok was deep in thought as he acknowledged his surrounding with absent-minded familiarity. Suddenly he realized he did not yet know the girl's name. It was the sort of thing that infuriated Vledder at times. DeKok firmly believed that useful information dried up with the appearance of an official form to fill out, or a too obvious taking of notes. All in good time, was his philosophy. But this was a good time to add to his sparse store of knowledge about the girl.

"How old are you?" he asked her.

"Ages."

"I'm not in the mood for riddles," he said sharply.

"Twenty, maybe." She shrugged her shoulders. "Or maybe twenty-one. I really don't know. It's been ages since I last celebrated a birthday."

DeKok snorted.

"But surely you know ..." He stopped, dropped the subject. "How long have you been in Amsterdam," he asked in a more sympathetic tone of voice.

"Since May of this year."

"And Colette?"

"The same."

"Where did you meet her?"

"On the highway." She made a vague gesture with her free arm. "Near the big clover-leaf at Bilthoven. We were hitchhiking."

DeKok nodded his understanding.

"Where are you from?"

She did not answer at once, but fingered the narrow necklace which hung down between her breasts.

"Breda," she said finally.

"And what's your name?"

"Marianne ... Marianne Vanburen." She made a comical gesture and gave a happy smile. "My father used to call me *Winnie the Pooh*. I used to be rather round, when I was little." Suddenly she looked up at the older man with a twinkle in her eyes. "What did they call you when you were small?" She hugged his arm intimately.

DeKok rubbed his face with a flat hand, trying to gain some time. The sudden candor of the young woman confused him, disturbed his equanimity.

"That ... I don't remember," he said moodily. "It was a long time ago."

She laughed heartily with a cheerful and guileless look on her face.

"I'll never forget Winnie the Pooh, if I live to be a hundred."

DeKok glanced at her. His face was serious.

"You don't seem very upset by Colette's death," he said.

The expression on her face sobered. She hung her head like an admonished child.

Meanwhile Vledder had turned a corner and they entered Emperor Street. The girl slowed her pace and looked at DeKok.

"Have you ever been *high*?"

"No." DeKok shook his head sadly. "No, not the way you mean."

She bit her lower lip and nodded resignedly.

"Colette was . . . high, I mean. That's all she ever wanted. She sacrificed everything for it."

"And what about you?"

Suddenly she was angry.

"Not me," she said vehemently. "I hold no truck with that filth. I don't want to be a slave . . . for nothing . . . of nobody."

She stopped and pointed at an abandoned building. A building slated to be demolished to make room for the subway. DeKok knew that some of these buildings were riddled with squatters, young people who came to Europe for the summer and ran out of money, or gambled it away, or spent it all on drugs. The influx of young people had started in the sixties with the so-called "hippies" and the "flower generation". In Amsterdam it had really never stopped. Some of them had lingered, now well into middle age, but they still dressed as if Woodstock had only happened yesterday. Some of the later arrivals had picked up the life-style and some had introduced a new life-style altogether. For a while there had been a predominance of leather jackets. These days sneakers seemed to be part of the "uniform". But in true Amsterdam tradition, every wave had left its adherents and newcomers were easily assimilated. Holland had always been the most tolerant country in the world and Amsterdam was probably the most tolerant city in the Netherlands. The Dutch would nod wisely. "*Iedere gek heeft zijn gebrek,*"* they would say to each other with a tolerant smile.

"There," she said tonelessly, "there it is."

The gray sleuth slightly tightened the pressure on her arm, willing her to walk with him. But she planted both feet firmly on the pavement and refused to budge.

"I'm not coming with you," she whispered.

DeKok released her arm and stood in front of her. With a tender gesture he wiped the hair out of her face and saw the fear in her eyes.

"Are you afraid?" he asked, surprised. "Afraid of a corpse?"

"No, not of Colette." She shook her head.

"Then . . . what are you afraid of?"

She did not answer.

DeKok put his arm around her and urged her forward. She resisted.

"I'd rather wait outside," she protested.

DeKok ignored her reluctance. Gently, but firmly he forced her forward. After a few paces she stopped again.

"Colette . . . she'll get a grave?"

"Isn't that what you came to see me about?"

She nodded and moved forward, dragging her feet. Without seeming to do so, DeKok remained alert, afraid she might bolt at the last minute.

They pushed open the door of the abandoned building. About two hundred years ago it must have been a substantial townhouse with large kitchens, a pantry and other service areas on the basement floor and servant's quarters in the attic. Today it

---

* Literally: *Every crazy person has his own particular delusion*, or: *Nobody's perfect*.

seemed to wait with eager anticipation for the wrecker's ball. The climbed the narrow, wooden staircase. The weakened wood creaked with every footstep. The girl stopped in the corridor on the third floor.

"Is this it?" asked DeKok.

She nodded, looking at the floor.

Vledder pushed open the door of the indicated room. The sickly sweet smell of a decomposing body greeted them. The young Inspector aimed his flashlight around the room. In a corner, underneath a boarded-up window, was a dirty mattress. There was a body on the mattress, covered with rags. DeKok stepped past Vledder and pulled away the rags. The pale face of a young woman became visible. Coagulated blood stuck to her hair, a wide open wound crossed her forehead.

Enraged, DeKok stripped the flashlight from Vledder's hand and aimed the beam full on Marianne's face.

"She's been murdered," he exclaimed angrily. "She didn't die a natural death."

"I never said that," was the calm answer.

DeKok felt himself losing control. It was one of those sudden rages that sometimes overcame the usually level-headed Dutch. Vledder knew the symptoms and was poised to intervene. DeKok, whose ancestors were Frisians, was subject to these sudden mood-swings, the last vestiges of the *beserker* rages that used to overcome the Vikings. It did not happen often and was seldom directed at a particular person, but Vledder took no chances.

DeKok gripped the girl by the shoulders and shook her violently.

"She's been murdered," he roared. "KILLED! You understand?"

The beautiful face of the young woman changed subtly. Her eyes narrowed and the dreamy look disappeared. Her full, sensuous lips compressed into a thin line. She looked twice her age and three times as callous. She pointed at the corpse.

"What difference does it make . . . to her?" Her voice was low and quivered with barely suppressed emotion.

DeKok released her. His anger washed away as suddenly as it had come over him. It left him drained and tired.

"To me," he said listlessly, "it makes all the difference in the world." He turned toward Vledder. "Take her back to the station and hold her. Tell *the Herd*. I'll be here."

2

With the flashlight to light his way, DeKok searched every nook and cranny of the room. He found a filthy, old hypodermic, crusts of molded bread, burned-off matches and cigarette butts. Blood had splattered the wall about three feet above the head of the victim. The blood covered the "I" and "F" of a hastily scrawled text: THIS IS THE FIRST DAY OF THE REST OF YOUR LIFE. The text stood out amid other, similar slogans, ranging from "Ban the Bomb" to "Freedom for Somalia". DeKok grinned without mirth. Youth had ever been in the forefront of that sort of demonstrations. It was relatively easy to discover what they were *against*, but harder to find out what they were *for*. But then, he admitted honestly, he was no different himself. In his youth he had violently opposed the drainage of the Zuyder Zee, from which his father used to gain his livelihood. As a cop he had been against the hierarchy, the red tape and injustice in the name of justice that was little more than thinly disguised expediency. In his own, stubborn way he *still* fought against injustice and complacency. Maybe being against something was not altogether negative, he reflected, after all, the greatest democracy in the world had been the result of a few colonists being against something. But at least, he was honest enough to admit, the Founding Fathers of the United States had presented the world with an alternative to what they were against. He was not at all sure that all of today's protesters had viable alternatives to offer.

He aimed his light at the corpse's face and a deep feeling of pity came over him. She was still so young . . . certainly less than twenty-five years. Her pale face looked sweet and gentle. Death had not been able to distort the expression. He pulled the rags further down and discovered to his amazement that her hands were devoutly folded on her breast, as if in prayer. If it had not been for the horrible wound, she would have looked peaceful. For just a moment his thoughts went back to a recent case. They had found another peaceful corpse, not too long ago. The man had also been murdered, albeit less obviously than this girl.

He closed his eyes, forced himself to be coolly observant. She had been left-handed. The left index finger and middle finger were nicotine stained. He took a few paces back and observed from a distance. The window, the blood on the wall, the mattress. She must have been in a seated position when the deadly blow had struck her. Then she slid diagonally against the wall. He looked closely at her clothes. They were old, dirty, but whole . . . no tears, no rips. There had not been a fight. The arms, bare to the shoulders, showed no bruises or lacerations. There were no injuries to the neck. In other words, no signs of a struggle.

The gray sleuth scratched the back of his neck. It was a strange murder. Why had the girl been struck? What was the motive? He pressed his lips together. Why did Marianne ask so specifically for a grave? Was she involved? Usually when somebody died in one of these abandoned buildings, everybody else would move out hastily, leaving the body for the wreckers to find. He decided to question Marianne closely.

He heard the diminishing sound of a siren and the screeching of brakes from outside. The first of the *Thundering*

Herd had arrived. It was DeKok's name for the small army of photographers, fingerprint experts, forensic specialists and other interested parties that flocked together at the scene of a violent death. An instant later Bram Weelen, the police photographer, blinked his eyes at DeKok's flashlight. Weelen pushed DeKok's hand aside and aimed his own flashlight at the scene, the oval spot of light came to rest on the face of the dead girl. The photographer grinned, unabashed.

"You're keeping charming company, I see, a sweet tete-a-tete with death."

"Death," admonished DeKok, "is seldom a tete-a-tete and *never* the subject of jokes."

Weelen would not be suppressed.

"You ever attended a seance?" he asked, ". . . the spirits are literally as thick as fleas." He placed his heavy bag on the floor and opened it. "Any special requests?" he asked as his busy fingers quickly checked his Hasselblad.

DeKok gestured sadly.

"A dirty old room. It's almost no use. Just give me the usual overviews and a few clear close-ups of the face. Maybe I'll need them. We don't know who she is, not for sure." He rubbed the bridge of his nose with a little finger. "Also get me a few shots of the outside of the building. If they tear it down in a few weeks, I've nothing left."

Weelen nodded.

There was renewed stumbling on the stairs and a few moments later DeKok greeted Dr. Koning, the Coroner. The old, eccentric doctor was still panting from his climb up the stairs.

"Good evening, doctor," said DeKok heartily.

The Coroner hardly took the time to lift his greenish Garibaldi hat.

"Where is it?" he asked gruffly.

DeKok stepped aside and aimed his flashlight at the corpse. The old doctor came closer and knelt next to the victim, ignoring Weelen's attempts to get a proper shot. For several seconds Dr. Koning looked at the corpse in silence. Then he looked over his shoulder.

"She's dead," he announced.

"Thank you, doctor," said DeKok seriously, his smile hidden behind the cone of light. He crouched down next to the old physician. "Would you be able to say anything about the cause of death?"

"No, no," answered the old man. "Dr. Rusteloos will tell you that, *after* the autopsy. You know I don't like to make statements that might influence the autopsy report." He glanced at DeKok and then relented. "The head-wound is definitely fatal," he admitted grudgingly, "*if* it was inflicted before she died."

"What about time of death, doctor?"

The coroner lifted the shoulders slightly and looked at the neck of the corpse.

"I estimate," he hesitated, "somewhere between two or three days ago."

"Thank you, doctor."

They both came back to their feet, two old men. It was unclear who supported whom. The small doctor looked at DeKok.

"Did I say good evening?" he asked.

DeKok looked sad and shook his head.

"Not yet, Doctor."

The old coroner grimaced. He could have looked hilarious in his formal, striped pants and old-fashioned tail-coat, with the half-glasses perched on the tip of his nose and his flamboyant Garibaldi hat covering his sparse hair. But the old Coroner was not a figure of fun. There was an aura of quiet competence about him, augmented by a certain old-fashioned formality and an undeniable sense of style.

"Well then, good evening," said the Coroner, as he shook DeKok's hand and left.

Weelen grinned soundlessly, adjusted something on his camera and suddenly the first flash showed the entire room momentarily in stark detail. Vledder returned. His entrance coincided with another flash from the Hasselblad and he was closely followed by Ben Kruger, the fingerprint expert.

"Another corpse?" queried Kruger. "Sometimes I think you deal in them wholesale." He looked with revulsion at the filthy room. "What a mess. What do you need me for?"

DeKok seemed puzzled.

"Fingers," he said finally.

Kruger spread both arms in a gesture of surrender.

"All right, all right," he complained. "But I tell you . . . even if they had killed the Queen in here . . ."

"It doesn't matter *who* gets killed," interrupted DeKok sharply. "We will do the best we can to find the killer."

"Yes, yes, of course," agreed Kruger soothingly. He knew that DeKok had a tendency to consider every murder as a personal affront. Vledder smiled to himself.

"See what you can do," interjected the young Inspector, "you're the expert. But if you think you can't . . ." He did not complete the sentence, but shrugged his shoulders. Meanwhile DeKok turned toward two attendants from the Coroner's office. The elder of the two men pointed at the corpse.

"Can we take her?" he asked.

"Just a moment," replied DeKok, "as soon as the photographer is finished."

Weelen looked up.

"Take her, as far as I'm concerned," he said nonchalantly. "I got everything I need." He pointed a shoulder at the mattress. "I'll take the close-ups tomorrow, before the autopsy."

The attendants placed the gurney on the floor and lifted the body into the body bag. Then they placed the bag on the gurney, secured it with a few straps and disappeared without saying another word. It seemed only seconds later when DeKok heard them slam the door of the "meat wagon". The sound touched DeKok. Again his glance was drawn to the text on the wall. *This is the first day of the rest of your life*, he read to himself. But not for Colette, he thought bitterly. There was no "rest" left for her and never again a "first" day.

Weelen hefted his bag and waved goodbye.

"You'll have the shots in the morning," he promised. "The close-ups will be a few hours later, after the autopsy."

DeKok nodded in his direction.

Ben Kruger was re-packing his jars and brushes.

"It's just plain hopeless," he sighed. "Everything is sticky with grease." He pointed with a melancholy gesture at the doorpost. "I wonder how long since somebody last washed the paint work. You *know* grease is the worst enemy of the self-respecting dactyloscopist."

DeKok could not suppress a grin. He knew all about Kruger's wife, the typical Dutch housewife who kept her husband's environment spotless. DeKok knew for a fact that she washed the windows every day and scrubbed the pavement outside their house at least twice a week with soap and water. She was the nicest and most hospitable woman one could imagine. DeKok had once attended a party at Kruger's house and the quantities of alcohol, coffee and food had assumed heroic proportions. Mrs. Kruger must have spent days in the kitchen, but half an hour after the last guests left, the house looked again like a showplace for an interior designer. His own wife drew the line at such excess zeal. She never washed the windows more than once a week.

"Why don't you ask your wife to stop by," suggested DeKok as Kruger was about to leave.

The fingerprint expert shook his head cheerlessly.

"No, I'd just as soon keep her away from my work. The poor soul doesn't know any better. She thinks that nothing is more important than cleaning." He shrugged his shoulders. "If I tell her that people actually live in places like this, she simply won't believe me." He shook hands with DeKok. "I'll be back tomorrow, when there's more light. Maybe I'll get lucky."

DeKok nodded agreement.

"Please don't forget to take the fingers of the victim. Maybe they'll be in your collection."

Vledder shivered. He knew that "fingers" was normal police jargon for fingerprints, but he always had a momentary vision of Kruger, wending his way through Amsterdam with a bag full of severed fingers.

"I'll do that," promised Kruger. "As a matter of fact, I'll make sure to be there when Weelen makes his close-ups. I'll take them then. What time will Dr. Rusteloos be there?"

"I don't know," answered DeKok, "I haven't spoken to him yet, but I guess in the afternoon."

"Fine," said Kruger. "I'll let you know right away if I find out something."

"They may know her at Narcotics," added Vledder thoughtfully.

Finally Vledder and DeKok remained alone. A patrol car with two uniformed constables, ready to seal the room as soon as the two detectives had left, remained in front of the building.

DeKok looked around the room once more, aided by the portable light that some constable had installed in a corner. He tried to visualize the room at the moment the murderer had struck the fatal blow, but he was not successful. The image would not solidify. The bare room had no supporting elements for his imagination. He looked at Vledder.

"What did you do with Marianne?"

"Put her in the Waiting Room."

"Did she say anything at all, while you were walking back?"

"Nothing special. She wanted to know if you ever had girlfriends."

"Me?"

"Yes."

The gray sleuth rubbed his flat hand across his face, hiding his embarrassment.

"She probably wanted to know how susceptible you were," volunteered Vledder. "But I assured her that you were a model husband."

"Thanks."

"She's something else, though," laughed Vledder. "You should have heard her with the desk-sergeant when he placed her in the Waiting Room. She ranted and raved . . . she must have woken up everybody in the cells below."

DeKok pushed his lower lip forward.

"Well, she'll have some explaining to do," he said. "She's the only possible witness we have so far and . . ."

Suddenly he stopped. There was a soft, almost imperceptible sound from somewhere. With one hand he switched off the portable light and placed the other on Vledder's arm, cautioning him to silence.

"What's the matter?" whispered Vledder.

"Somebody's here."

"Where?"

"Here . . . somewhere."

They remained silent, stood absolutely still. Then they both heard the sound. It came from the right. Carefully, balancing on the balls of his feet, DeKok crept closer. He switched on his flashlight and stared at a blank wall. With sudden inspiration he rushed soundlessly into the corridor and found a closet door. He opened the door with a quick movement and aimed the beam of his light inside. On the floor of the closet was a cardboard box, filled with rags. A child rested on the rags. It waved small arms, made gurgling sounds and blinked at the light.

3

For a few seconds DeKok was speechless, then he leaned forward and lifted the child from the box. Carefully he cradled it in his arms.

"A boy," grinned Vledder, confused, "It's a boy."

DeKok gave him a withering look.

"Your knowledge of biology astounds me," he said evenly. The child in his arms crowed with pleasure.

Vledder laughed out loud.

"He understands you," he said, surprise in his voice. "He does."

DeKok lifted the child in both hands and held it away from himself.

"How old do you think he is?"

"Two years?" The young Inspector shrugged his shoulders. "I've no idea. Does he have teeth?"

"Teeth?"

"Children, you see," explained Vledder didactically, "are never *born* with teeth."

DeKok again cradled the baby in his arms and carefully inserted his little finger into the tiny mouth. He nodded slowly to himself.

"I can feel them," he said solemnly. "Mostly up front, quite a few." He removed his finger and took some rags from the box. He gave the baby to Vledder to hold and wrapped the child as best as he could. "The night air can be dangerous," he divulged.

Vledder nodded with a worried look on his face.

"What are we going to do with him?"

"Take him with us, of course," said DeKok, surprise in his voice.

"To the station?"

"What else? We can hardly leave him here."

"Then what?"

"What *do* you mean?"

"We're not a kindergarten," laughed Vledder nervously. "You can't keep him at the station."

"No," said DeKok pensively. "You're right. That's impossible." He scratched the back of his neck. "We'll have to do something about that." He played his flashlight through the interior of the closet. "Just put him back in the box for now. There's another floor above here and we haven't yet taken a look there."

Vledder kneeled down and placed the little boy carefully back in the box. The instant he let go of the child, however, he started to cry. DeKok looked down on them.

"You're hurting him," he said severely.

"I didn't do a thing," protested Vledder.

"Then why is he crying?"

"He doesn't want to go back in the closet." Vledder rose, the child in his arms. DeKok handed him his flashlight and took the bundle from his young colleague.

"Here, you take a quick look upstairs and I'll wait here."

Vledder rushed away and was back within minutes.

"Empty," he reported. "No floors, no walls, nothing. Just the beams."

DeKok nodded his understanding. He shifted the bundle and allowed the baby to rest against his shoulder. Slowly they descended the stairs.

They nodded to the constables, who went upstairs to seal off the premises. The forensic team would come later, or perhaps in the morning. They walked back to the station, taking shortcuts only DeKok knew. Near the bridge toward Old Church Square they encountered a group of prostitutes. DeKok increased his pace, afraid of becoming the center of attention for a group of simpering whores. He knew about their sentimentality, their particular affection for young children. One of them called after them. DeKok recognized the voice of Black Josie and quickened his step some more.

A few cops stood in front of the desk-sergeant. They eyed the two detectives strangely when they arrived with the baby. When the Watch-Commander saw them, he emerged from his cubby-hole.

"I'm glad you're here," he said, relief in his voice while he pointed a thumb over his shoulder. "She wants to go home."

"She'll have to be patient a little longer," said DeKok calmly.

The Watch-Commander looked at the child.

"Where did you get that?" he asked.

DeKok looked over his shoulder and saw that the constables had drawn near, eager to hear DeKok's explanation.

"Found it," he said and disappeared in the direction of the stairs to the detective room.

Vledder followed close behind.

In the detective room, DeKok placed the child carefully on his desk. He took the rags away and looked the child over. A good looking boy, he concluded, strong, with a milk-white skin, blond hair and clear blue eyes in a happy face. He was dressed in a white cotton sweater and nothing else. He looked well-fed.

The sleuth leaned forward. His craggy face, with the expression of a good-natured boxer, did not seem to frighten the child. He smiled happily at the man with the gray hair.

"Where's Mama?" asked DeKok.

The little boy chuckled as if DeKok had said something funny. He waved with both hands.

"Mama out."

DeKok smiled, enchanted by the little boy.

"Where's Papa?"

"Papa out."

"Where's Oma?"

"Oma out."

"Where's Opa?"

"Opa out."*

Young Vledder laughed out loud.

"All out," he joked, "All gone."

DeKok persisted, unperturbed.

"Where's Brother?" he coaxed.

The child did not react but stared at him.

"Where's Sis?"

A faint smile played around the baby's lips, but there was incomprehension in the startling blue eyes.

DeKok paused, then he playfully tickled one of the rosy cheeks with a thick finger.

"Where's Mama?" he asked again.

This time the little boy reacted confused, scared.

"Mama out."

It did not sound the same as last time. There was a definite note of discomfort, perhaps fear.

"Mama out," repeated the child, "Mama out."

Vledder shook his head disapprovingly.

---

* *Opa* and *Oma*, literally "old pa" and "old ma", the way in which Dutch children address their grandparents.

"You better stop, you're scaring the little tyke."

DeKok turned toward the young Inspector, keeping one eye on the child. His face was serious and the look of a good-natured boxer had disappeared to be replaced with the grim visage of a bulldog.

"Get Marianne up here."

When Vledder had left, he gave it one more try. His face softened as he leaned over the little boy.

"Where's Papa?" he asked gently.

The kid pulled a lip and started to cry.

"Papa out . . . Papa out."

DeKok released a deep sigh. He lifted the little boy from the desk and placed him on the floor. He looked around, a scared look on his face, a finger in his tiny mouth. He took a few hesitant steps and flopped on his bare behind. Shocked, DeKok rushed over. The child looked surprised and then started to bawl . . . loud and penetrating. A number of detectives looked up momentarily, but some did not even acknowledge the sound. One more sound in the room could hardly distract them. A suspect, hand-cuffed to a chair, looked around and grinned. DeKok picked up the child, cradled him in his arms and made soothing noises. It did not work. On the contrary, the child switched into high gear and the noise increased.

Suddenly the door of the room opened and Marianne Vanburen stormed into the room, straight for the child. Her eyes flashed as she took the child from DeKok. The little boy immediately became quiet.

"What did they do to you?" she asked, comforting the baby by rocking it slightly. "What did they do to you?" She gave DeKok an accusing look, anger in her eyes. "Why didn't you leave him in his box in the closet?"

The old man ignored the remark. He pointed a finger at the child.

"Your child?"

Marianne did not answer. She rocked the baby in a sweet cadence, executing small dance steps while she crooned to him.

"Is that your child?" insisted DeKok.

"Colette's" she said curtly, shaking her head.

"Was Colette married?"

"No?"

"Who's the father?"

She stuck her chin out, a challenging look in her blue eyes.

"Is that important?"

"Children," shrugged DeKok, "always have a father."

She stepped closer.

"Not Bobby, Bobby only has an procreator."

"All right," said DeKok resignedly, "who's the procreator?"

She shook her head and smirked contemptuously.

"You . . . you can only think in sterile terms, can't you?" She wiped the back of her free hand across her forehead and snorted. "Inspector," she jeered. "Legal guardian of middle class morality." She paused, took a deep breath. "What do *you* know about it! Can't you imagine that a girl goes with a man just because . . . because she wants some warmth, some tenderness."

"I can imagine that," he answered calmly.

"Colette needed warmth." She caressed the child's head.

DeKok nodded his understanding. He took a chair and held it for her with old-world charm, willing her to relax.

"And then Bobby came?"

She sat down with the child in her lap and shrugged her shoulders, as if dismissing a menial.

"He came . . . so what?"

"No abortion?"

"No, Colette wanted the child."

"Where?"

"Where?" she repeated, apparently not understanding the question.

"Where was Bobby born?"

She hesitated, flicked her tongue along her lips, swallowed. "That . . . eh, I . . . I don't know. Colette never told me."

DeKok cocked his head at her and locked his eyes into hers.

"Why didn't Colette stay with her parents?"

Suddenly Marianne reacted sharply. Again she snorted.

"Parents!" It sounded like a curse. All her contempt was contained in that single word. "If the child happens to make something of himself, they pat each other on the back and take all the credit. But if their so-called pedagogy fails, the failed product is chased out of the house."

DeKok rubbed his face with a tired gesture. He had no inclination for a debate about the raising of children. The girl hardly seemed capable of objectivity.

"Colette," he said carefully, "had a child and left Utrecht."

"I guess so." She made a helpless gesture.

"Did she have the child with her when you met her near Bilthoven?"

Marianne nodded.

"She carried Bobby in a back-pack, a baby carrier on her back."

"And you stayed together since then?"

"Yes. More or less by accident. We hitchhiked to Amsterdam and moved into the abandoned building. We'd heard from some guys around the monument that there was room and that the police never checked."

"What did you live on?"

She moved uneasily in her chair and grinned cheerlessly.

"Stealing, what else. Stores, warehouses and supermarkets, the docks, whatever."

"Never been caught?"

"Just once," her face fell, she smiled sadly. "In the *Beehive*. We didn't have much. They let us go."

The largest department store in Amsterdam would, thought DeKok. They would rather move the thieves quietly out of the store than make a scene. It was bad for the tourist trade. He smiled grimly. The fact that the perpetrators had been two young, attractive girls, would have had something to do with it as well.

"And was it enough?" he asked.

"What?"

"The thefts . . . was it enough to live on?"

"Not always. Sometimes we picked up a guy."

"For money?"

She lowered her head. The long hair fell forward and shielded her and the child. The child thought it was a game and grabbed for the hair. She did not seem to notice.

"Only in an emergency," she whispered.

"Who took care of Bobby, then?"

She lifted her head and showed her fine, oval face with the striking blue eyes.

"I . . . I took care of Bobby. Especially during the last few weeks when Colette was more and more under the influence of drugs." A tear dribbled down her cheek. She placed the child on the edge of the desk and wiped her eyes with the hem of her skirt. "It doesn't matter. She would have died anyway, Colette . . . tomorrow, the day after or next week. She was in bad shape and getting worse. You could see it. Death had already marked her, the shadow hovered over her."

DeKok listened carefully to her tone of voice, seeking to determine the degree of sincerity. It was difficult to analyze the girl's reactions. They were strange, different.

"Somebody bashed in her head," he said, more sharply than he had intended.

She stared into the distance, absent-mindedly balancing the child on the edge of the desk, keeping him steady.

"It was two days ago," she said softly. She hesitated, reflected. "Maybe three days ago . . . yes, three days ago. I came home and I had bread and sausage and a box of Graham crackers for Bobby. Colette was on the mattress, leaning against the wall. There was blood on her face, her head. I put down the groceries and came closer. 'Colette,' I said, 'Colette.' She had her eyes open, but she didn't see anymore. There was no light in the eyes, no life. That's when I knew she was dead."

She shuddered, stroked the child's head.

"I was completely at a loss. I sat down next to her on the mattress and held her hand and prayed . . . Our Father, what I could remember of it." She paused. The blue eyes again filled with tears. "I don't know how long I sat next to her. When it got dark, I put her down on her back and folded her hands."

"Then what?"

She looked at him, a vacant stare in her eyes.

"I gave Bobby some crackers." She hugged the child. "He was so good. He knew, really, he understood what had happened to Colette. I put him in his box. When he was asleep, I took my tambourine and went out."

"To . . . eh, to dance?"

"To dance." She nodded slowly. "Yes, to dance. You see . . . I *had* to. It was the only way for me . . . to absorb it . . . to help myself get back to reality. I can't remember what I did that night. I think I just walked and danced. When it got light, I went back to take care of Bobby. Colette looked really peaceful on her mattress, as if she was asleep. She was so beautiful that way. I had never known her to be that beautiful. I remained next to her, all day, on a pillow on the floor. That night I went out again. The next day I was back."

"Didn't anybody else show up"

"No."

"Why didn't you go to the police?"

"I wasn't finished."

"With what?"

"With her death. I had not been able to absorb it as yet, was unable to deal with it. I couldn't fathom it. The reality just didn't penetrate. After two days I realized that it might take some time. That's why I wanted a grave for her."

DeKok rubbed the bridge of his nose with a little finger. Then he rubbed the corners of his eyes with a thumb and middle finger. It was a tired, exhausted gesture.

"Have you any idea," he asked listlessly, "why she was murdered?"

She looked at him.

"Ask her killer."

DeKok was still capable of surprise. He looked at her, gauged the expression on her face. Something in her voice warned him, urged him to be careful, alert.

"You know the killer?"

"Yes," she nodded almost imperceptibly. "The man who took the koala."

"Koala?"

She pulled the child off the desk, held him in her lap. With a tender movement she cradled him against her breast.

"Bobby's little bear."

4

Vledder slapped his forehead with the heel of his hand.

"That girl is crazy," he exclaimed vehemently, "just plain loco! I've never met anybody as weird as that."

DeKok pursed his lips.

"I think," he said thoughtfully, "that Marianne Vanburen is a lot smarter than we give her credit for. Her thought processes do not run according to the familiar patterns we're used to. That's why she seems a bit strange."

"Oh yeah?" snorted Vledder. "But who, in their right mind, takes to the street with a tambourine, to go dancing, when her friend has just been killed?"

"Ah, well," shrugged DeKok, "some people drown their sorrows in liquor and others may try to forget by dancing. Who can say?"

"She's a peculiar girl," said Vledder, shaking his head. "Very peculiar, to say the least. You think Major Bossart will take her in?"

"At least for the time being," considered DeKok. "The Major promised to look after her. There's always a place for a lost sheep, according to the Major." He smiled. "The Salvation Army has been a source of succor for some time."

The young Inspector pointed at the child, wrapped in DeKok's raincoat and fast asleep on top of the desk. DeKok had finally found a use for his computer terminal. He had pushed it around to provide a shadow to protect the sleeping child's face from the harsh glare of the overhead lights.

"What are we going to do with Bobby?"

"We'll take him to the Sisters in Warmoes Street."

"Sisters . . . what sisters?" Vledder looked perplexed.

"My very dear friends . . ." DeKok made a grand gesture. ". . . the Sisters Augustine de Saint Monica. You hardly ever hear about them, they prefer to hide their light under a bushel. But they do good work and I've never called on them in vain."

"Do they take in children?"

"In special cases, like this . . . sure. We'll have to research Colette's family relations, of course, and before a final disposition can be made, we'll have to inform the Juvenile Protection Agency."

The young Inspector sank back in his chair.

"We're in a nice spot. A young child, almost a baby . . . a perfect witness. And a murder without a motive."

"Who says so?" inquired DeKok blandly.

"Without a motive," repeated Vledder. "Do you really believe that Colette was killed for a toy koala?"

"Why not? It, in itself, *could* have been a motive."

"A coupla bucks?" Vledder grinned broadly, there was sarcasm in his voice. "The stores are full of those things. You can get them everywhere. Stuffed toys . . . hardly a rarity."

DeKok scratched the back of his neck.

"Perhaps," he speculated, ""the murderer wasn't after the little bear at all."

For a moment Vledder looked confused. Then he suddenly sat up straight and looked wide-eyed at his older partner.

"Of course . . . not the toy . . . . but the stuffing. Heroin . . . the little bear was stuffed with heroin. You understand?" Careful not to wake the sleeping child, he came closer to DeKok and whispered urgently: "You see? Colette was an addict, used heroin. She had no money to buy it . . . so what did she have to do to feed her habit?"

"Deal?"

"Exactly." Vledder nodded emphatically. "Deal! She became a dealer to help feed her habit. But when you're a dealer, you need a supply, a supply you can't afford to carry around for everybody to see. You have to hide it . . ." He paused, pointed at the sleeping child. "Hide it in a child's toy."

DeKok looked serious.

"It's a reasonable assumption," he agreed. "Tomorrow we'll have to ask Marianne how Colette obtained her drugs . . . who she knew in the drug world."

Once Vledder took hold of a theory, he became fully committed to it. It was part of his nature to be precipitous. Vledder still looked at the world in stark demarcations of black and white, good and evil, criminal and law-abiding, "them and us". DeKok, with the experience of years, was less certain of himself. He had long since come to the conclusion that the world consisted of various shades of gray. There was a little good in the worst people and a little evil in the best. Although he did not reject Vledder's theory out of hand, he was not at all convinced that it would be the right conclusion, or for that matter, the only possibility. But Vledder was not to be denied.

"That's it," he whispered enthusiastically. "Believe me, *that's* the motive . . . heroin. Why else would somebody want to kill a girl like that . . . for her money?"

Before DeKok had a chance to answer that question, he noticed the door of the detective room being opened. A large, heavy woman approached DeKok's desk. Her face was red with exertion as she made her away across the room. DeKok recognized her at once: Josephine Kraaienberg, better known as Black Josie. He came from behind his desk and held a chair for her.

"Please sit down," he said in a friendly voice. "What can I do for you?"

Her high, firm bosom heaved, threatening to burst from her dress.

"I couldn't come sooner," she said in a hoarse, sensual voice. "I had a late client." She wiped the sweat from her forehead with a dainty handkerchief. "Bothersome little man... all sorts of special wishes, but no cash."

"And?" asked DeKok, shaking his head in sympathy.

"I saw you with the child," she said, indicating the sleeping Bobby. "I called after you."

"I didn't hear you," lied DeKok with a sad face.

"You finally took it away from them?"

"Took it away?"

"Yes, of course, it was a disgrace."

"What?"

"Those dirty bitches," she said angrily, gesturing vaguely toward the window. "They've been peddling the child for weeks."

"Peddling?" DeKok was surprised and showed it.

Black Josie nodded, her face quivered with indignation.

"They offered the poor thing for sale. They approached a number of us girls."

* * *

Inspector Vledder was reading from his ubiquitous note book.

"Colette Maesen," he read, "was born in Utrecht, twenty-four years ago. She was the second child in a family of moderate means. Father, now pensioned, was an engineer for the Dutch Railways. Mother worked as a window dresser in a department store, before her marriage." He flipped a page. "Colette went to High School but was permanently suspended at age seventeen for improper behavior. She found a job with an agency supplying temporary labor. She didn't like the job and there were problems in the work environment. There were also arguments at home. Two months after she had been suspended, she left home. The parents filed a missing person report. Two years after that, she was sentenced to one month in jail after having been convicted of shoplifting." The young Inspector closed his book. "That's all we have on her. There are no further reports."

DeKok looked with admiration at his young partner.

"How did you find that out so fast?"

Vledder pointed smugly at the telephone.

"I called Juvenile Police in Utrecht. One of the guys I went to the Academy with works there. He told me that there were a number of 'runaway' reports after the first one. Apparently she started with drugs while still in High School. That's when the trouble started. Until that time she was a model student."

"What about the older sister?"

"Graduated near the top of her class. She's been described as having above average intelligence."

"And the second went adrift," nodded DeKok. "A familiar picture, it happens more often than we care to admit. Anything known about her relations with men?"

"She led a rather loose life from an early age. Nothing is known about any regular attachments. No names, anyway."

"Her parents are still alive?"

"Sure, both of them. They're in their sixties."

"When has the autopsy been scheduled?"

"At three this afternoon."

"Then have the parents come this morning. It will be better for them to officially identify the body, *before* the autopsy. She looks bad enough and may look worse after Dr. Rusteloos is finished with her. Also ask for the older sister to come and . . . if possible . . . somebody who knew Colette but isn't a family member."

Vledder looked at his watch and calculated quickly.

"About noon, that all right with you?"

DeKok nodded agreement and leaned against the backrest of his chair.

"When was Bobby born?"

"Unknown in the Utrecht Register. Three years ago she was recorded as having moved to Amsterdam."

"Amsterdam?" asked DeKok, a puzzled look on his face.

Vledder flipped through his notebook.

"Yes, here it is. Upon arrival in Amsterdam she was registered as living at 112 Saint Jacob Street."

"Did you check that out?"

Vledder made an apologetic gesture.

"Haven't got that far, yet."

They were interrupted by the phone. Vledder reached out and lifted the receiver. He listened and then replaced the receiver carefully. He gave DeKok a peculiar look.

"The Commissaris* wants to see you."

* * *

Commissaris Buitendam, the tall, stately Chief of Warmoes Street Station always looked out of place. Warmoes Street was

---

* Commissaris: a rank equivalent to Captain. There are only two ranks higher: Chief-Commissaris and Chief Constable. Each jurisdiction has only a single Chief Constable, the highest possible police rank. There is one Chief Constable for all of Amsterdam. Other ranks in the Municipal Police are: Constable, Constable First Class, Sergeant, Adjutant, Inspector, Chief-Inspector and Commissaris. Adjutants and below are equivalent to non-commissioned ranks. Inspector is a rank equivalent to 2nd Lieutenant.

moderate means. Father, now pensioned, was an engineer for the Dutch Railways. Mother worked as a window dresser in a department store, before her marriage." He flipped a page. "Colette went to High School but was permanently suspended at age seventeen for improper behavior. She found a job with an agency supplying temporary labor. She didn't like the job and there were problems in the work environment. There were also arguments at home. Two months after she had been suspended, she left home. The parents filed a missing person report. Two years after that, she was sentenced to one month in jail after having been convicted of shoplifting." The young Inspector closed his book. "That's all we have on her. There are no further reports."

DeKok looked with admiration at his young partner.

"How did you find that out so fast?"

Vledder pointed smugly at the telephone.

"I called Juvenile Police in Utrecht. One of the guys I went to the Academy with works there. He told me that there were a number of 'runaway' reports after the first one. Apparently she started with drugs while still in High School. That's when the trouble started. Until that time she was a model student."

"What about the older sister?"

"Graduated near the top of her class. She's been described as having above average intelligence."

"And the second went adrift," nodded DeKok. "A familiar picture, it happens more often than we care to admit. Anything known about her relations with men?"

"She led a rather loose life from an early age. Nothing is known about any regular attachments. No names, anyway."

"Her parents are still alive?"

"Sure, both of them. They're in their sixties."

"When has the autopsy been scheduled?"

"At three this afternoon."

"Then have the parents come this morning. It will be better for them to officially identify the body, *before* the autopsy. She looks bad enough and may look worse after Dr. Rusteloos is finished with her. Also ask for the older sister to come and . . . if possible . . . somebody who knew Colette but isn't a family member."

Vledder looked at his watch and calculated quickly.

"About noon, that all right with you?"

DeKok nodded agreement and leaned against the backrest of his chair.

"When was Bobby born?"

"Unknown in the Utrecht Register. Three years ago she was recorded as having moved to Amsterdam."

"Amsterdam?" asked DeKok, a puzzled look on his face.

Vledder flipped through his notebook.

"Yes, here it is. Upon arrival in Amsterdam she was registered as living at 112 Saint Jacob Street."

"Did you check that out?"

Vledder made an apologetic gesture.

"Haven't got that far, yet."

They were interrupted by the phone. Vledder reached out and lifted the receiver. He listened and then replaced the receiver carefully. He gave DeKok a peculiar look.

"The Commissaris* wants to see you."

* * *

Commissaris Buitendam, the tall, stately Chief of Warmoes Street Station always looked out of place. Warmoes Street was

---

* Commissaris: a rank equivalent to Captain. There are only two ranks higher: Chief-Commissaris and Chief Constable. Each jurisdiction has only a single Chief Constable, the highest possible police rank. There is one Chief Constable for all of Amsterdam. Other ranks in the Municipal Police are: Constable, Constable First Class, Sergeant, Adjutant, Inspector, Chief-Inspector and Commissaris. Adjutants and below are equivalent to non-commissioned ranks. Inspector is a rank equivalent to 2nd Lieutenant.

known among police officers as "the Dutch Hill Street" and the Commissaris looked and spoke like a diplomat more at home in the League of Nations than on the edge of the Red Light District. He waved with a narrow hand, an amicable expression on his pale face.

"Sit down, DeKok," he said in a cheerful, friendly voice. "About that killing in Emperor Street, the homeless girl . . . your case?"

"Colette Maesen," nodded DeKok.

"Oh . . . Colette Maesen . . . is that her name?"

DeKok scratched the side of his nose.

"Colette with double t and Maesen with ae," he amplified.

The Commissaris wrote down the name.

"She was a drug addict?"

"Heroin."

"You expect any complications?"

DeKok looked at him. There was a look of incomprehension on his face.

"How . . . how do you mean?" he asked suspiciously.

The Commissaris gestured impatiently.

"Pieces in the paper . . . difficulties with the family. You know what I mean." He pursed his lips, considering. "After all, DeKok, it isn't exactly an unusual case." There was a hint of contempt in his voice. "It isn't the first time that an addict has been found in an abandoned building."

"It was murder," stated DeKok evenly.

"Certainly, certainly," the Commissaris said reasonably. "And it must be investigated, of course." He tried a charming smile. "But I wouldn't make it too complicated, were I you. Surely the investigation can be wrapped up in a few days. After all, we have more important cases."

DeKok narrowed his eyes. He felt the anger rising in himself, but he controlled it with an effort. This type of situation and DeKok's usual reaction to it, went a long way to explain why he would probably never be promoted above his present rank.

"This murder is not important?" he asked icily. "The death of an insignificant homeless girl is not worth the trouble?"

The Commissaris jumped up.

"I didn't formulate it that way, DeKok," he said severely.

"No," answered DeKok, grinning in a way calculated to infuriate. "No, I formulated it that way . . . just to be clear about it." He shook his head in commiseration. "After all, you wouldn't want there to be any misunderstandings between us, would you?"

The Chief lost his temper. Angry red spots appeared on the commissarial cheeks. His hands shook.

"I don't appreciate your sarcasm, DeKok," he said furiously.

The gray sleuth made a resigned gesture.

"I suspected as much," he said calmly. He stood up. "Unless you have further important communications . . . there's a lot of work involved with a murder investigation."

The Commissaris shook over his whole body. He stretched an arm out in the direction of the door.

"OUT!" he roared.

DeKok left.

5

Vledder shook his head when DeKok returned.

"Same story again?" he asked laughingly. "I don't know why the two of you go through the same exercise over and over again. By now you should know ... he thinks one way and you're opposite. Just listen to him and let it slide. You know you can't be fired and in the end he always leaves you alone. He just wants information."

DeKok rubbed the bridge of his nose with a little finger.

"Just because we're dealing with a homeless girl, a girl nobody cares about, we're supposed to wrap it up in a few days." His voice shook with indignation and he shook his head with a stubborn expression on his face. "No ... I can't do that. I'll find her killer, if it takes all year."

Young Vledder looked at the familiar face and realized that DeKok was serious. This was not the time to shrug off the Chief's words with a few joking, soothing remarks. The young man hated those confrontations, especially since DeKok, in an unguarded moment had revealed that he and the Commissaris had attended the Police Academy at the same time. DeKok had become a cop and remained a cop, protecting the public and fighting for justice in his own peculiar ways. The Commissaris, so it seemed, had developed into a politician, worried about appearances and his pension.

"I agree," said Vledder and gestured with his head. "There's a woman waiting for you in the interrogation room... a certain Hendrika Beerfleet."

"Squinting Rika?"

Vledder grinned sheepishly.

"I don't know that. She *does* seem to be a bit cross-eyed. She said that Black Josie had sent her."

DeKok ambled in the direction of the interrogation room. Squinting Rika was an aging prostitute and DeKok had known her for as long as he had been assigned to Warmoes Street Station. Twenty years, or more, he reflected. He tried to imagine how Rika had looked twenty some years ago. He couldn't remember. He opened the door of the little room and smiled.

"Hello Rika, my dear," he said heartily. "And to what do I owe the honor?"

She looked at him and giggled.

"Honor ... listen to that! I just wanted you to know that they offered the child to me as well."

DeKok sat down across from her.

"How did that happen?"

Squinting Rika moved in her chair, trying to find a more comfortable position on the hard, institutional furniture.

"Well ... eh, they came to see me."

"Who?"

"Those two girls from Emperor Street and a guy."

"A guy?"

"Yes, a wimp really. You know what I mean ... long, dirty hair, a straggly beard, an army jacket and jeans and sneakers, of course. Skinny, about thirty ... should have known better."

DeKok nodded. Rika's assessment of a man would more than likely be to the point.

"What did they say?"

"They wanted to know if I wanted to buy the child."

"Did they mention a price?"

"No." She shook her head. "They never mentioned a price. It never got that far. I couldn't care less about other people's children. What would I want with them? I've three of my own."

"Did they show you the child?"

"Oh, yes. A blond little boy, about one and a half, two years old. They asked me what he was worth to me. I mean to tell you, I was flabbergasted. Let's face it, it doesn't happen every day that you're offered a child for sale. I told them they'd never get away with it. The Juvenile Protection Agency and the Children's Police will nab you before you can say illegal adoption procedures. Then the guy opened his mouth and said it wouldn't happen with *that* child. I just couldn't deduct him from the taxes, or expect a child's allowance."

DeKok's eyebrows rippled dangerously.

"Is that what he said?"

Rika did not see the movement of the eyebrows. She placed her middle finger and index finger on her closed eyes.

"By the light in my eyes, DeKok, I swear it."

* * *

The gray sleuth threw his accusations in her face, vehemently, angrily, cruelly with sharp, hurting words. His usually so friendly face looked like a thundercloud. Marianne Vanburen raised both arms in a defensive gesture.

"It's a lie," she hissed, "pure slander. Those women are making it up. We didn't want to sell Bobby. That was never our intention."

"Then what was?"

"We wanted to find him a temporary home."

"But you asked for money," interrupted Vledder.

"It was a test," she said, shaking her head with irritation. "Just a test, no more. We knew that whores usually take good care of their children and we wanted the best for Bobby. That's why we asked how much the child would be worth to them. Whoever offered the most, would have received Bobby on a temporary basis. That's where he would have been best off . . ."

"And the money?"

She shrugged her shoulders, a tired gesture.

"It wasn't about money at all," she said, irked. "I told you that. It was an emergency measure. We had to get rid of the child. It wasn't fair to hold on to him. What could we offer him in that old building . . . that could be torn down around our ears before we knew it. We couldn't keep him forever in that hall-closet."

DeKok thoughtfully rubbed his chin.

"I still have problems understanding you," he said softly. "Colette must have carried the child around for almost two years, you were staying in that building for several months and then, all of a sudden, you want to find another home for the child?" He gave her a penetrating look. "Had something else happened?"

"Colette," sighed Marianne. "It was Colette. She no longer saw a future . . . for herself, you understand? Despite her addiction she had lucid moments and then she realized that she wouldn't be able to take care of Bobby much longer. She *knew* she didn't have much longer to live."

"Then why," asked DeKok, spreading wide his arms, "didn't she just find a regular home? That's one of the functions of the Juvenile Protection Agency. There are other organizations as well."

"Organizations," snorted Marianne. "That's the whole problem . . . organizations, institutions." She snorted again. "I *hate* institutions. I hate all officialdom. Bobby in some sort of orphanage?" She shook her head emphatically. "Never, you hear me, never! The in - sti - tu - tion - al raising of children, bah!" Her voice shook. "They turn out wrecks . . . human wrecks, that's all!"

"I know some orphans," said DeKok mildly, "who have achieved quite a bit in society."

She laughed denigratingly.

"Sure you do. You know how? Because they are driven by an inferiority complex." She stood up and leaned her hands on the desk as she brought her face close to his. "You ever heard of collective love, institutionalized love? Of course not, because it doesn't exist. You can love another human being, perhaps two or three . . . but you can't love whole tribes of people. A child should not, *must* not be raised in an institution. There's not enough love, not enough interest . . . . not enough care!" She sank back in her chair, her face was pale, drawn. "Where's Bobby now?" she asked softly.

"With the Augustine Sisters in Warmoes Street."

"Are they taking care of him?"

DeKok nodded, smiling.

"Oh yes, they're taking care of him, loving him. It's a matter of some concern if he'll be able to withstand the surfeit of love he's receiving. Sometimes he has twenty mothers at the same time."

She looked at him, weighed his words.

"I hope for your sake, you're right." There was a hint of a threat in her voice. She stood up and left the room without a word. DeKok called her back.

"Who was the young man who was with you?"

"You mean Fred?"

DeKok shrugged his shoulders.

"Long hair, scraggly beard, jeans and sneakers."

"I know about three dozen like that."

DeKok's face remained expressionless.

"He was with you," he said patiently, "when you offered the child."

"Fred . . . Fred Mellenkamp. He studied Law."

"I see . . . and he gave you legal advice . . . when you were selling Bobby?"

She banged the desk with her small fist. Her eyes flashed.

"It wasn't a sale!"

DeKok made an apologetic gesture.

"Did he give legal advice?" he persisted.

She sat down again, shook her head.

"No, he was just there. That's all."

"Is Fred your friend . . . or Colette's?"

She looked up, a challenge in her eyes.

"What do you mean? . . . sometimes I slept with him, if that's what you mean."

DeKok ignored the remark. It seemed as if he had forgotten her altogether while he searched his pockets. He finally found a toffee in a hip pocket and slowly removed the wrapper. Without looking at her, he placed the sweet in his mouth and chewed thoughtfully.

"Did Fred take the koala?" The question was sudden, totally unexpected.

Marianne Vanburen froze. She stared at the old man, fear in her eyes. Then she shook her head with short, nervous movements.

"Not Fred," she panted. "Fred didn't do it. He didn't kill Colette."

* * *

DeKok looked somber. Almost shyly he reached out his hand to the old couple.

"Condolences," he said softly, "my deepest sympathy for the loss of your daughter. You will understand, it is painful for us as well, to have to ask you to see her under the present circumstances." He made an apologetic gesture. "I would have liked to spare you this ordeal."

"In a way I'm not surprised," said the woman, a bit waspishly. "I've said it again and again . . . she'll come to a bad end." She gestured toward her husband. "Henk never bothered about it. He always said that a good child manages herself." She shook her head. "Colette couldn't manage a thing, least of all her own life."

DeKok pulled up an extra chair and invited the couple to sit down.

"You mean," he said blandly, "that Colette was a good child, but unable to control herself?"

A sad smile appeared on the old woman's face.

"That's exactly it, sir," she agreed. "Yessir, that's it. Anybody could influence Colette, she was putty in their hands. It all depended on what sort of hands she fell into." Again she gestured toward her husband. "As far as that's concerned, she had the same personality as my husband."

DeKok smiled encouragingly.

"But he . . . eh, wound up in good hands?"

The remark visibly flattered her.

"In the beginning we had some difficult times. His mother was a witch, who . . ."

The old man moved uneasily in his chair.

"You shouldn't say that about Mother. The old woman . . ."

DeKok interrupted hastily.

"When did you see Colette last?"

"At least two years ago."

"Where?"

"Here, in Amsterdam. She lived in a small street not far from here."

"Alone?"

"What do you mean?"

"Did she live by herself?"

"No." The old woman shook her head. "No, she lived with some sort of artist, a painter ... Karel Karsemeyer. I have a picture of him." She searched through her purse and found a wrinkled photograph. "That's him ... Karel."

DeKok accepted the picture and looked at it with some interest. He saw a man with a full beard and a painter's palette in one hand.

"Is this Bobby's father?" When he saw the incomprehension in the woman's eyes, he explained further. "Bobby, Colette's child ... was the painter the father?"

"A child ... does Colette have a child?" The woman seemed genuinely astonished.

"Yes," nodded DeKok, "didn't you know?"

Her mouth fell open.

"No, I never ... I never knew," she stammered, completely taken aback. "A child ... what kind of child?"

"A little boy ... about one and a half, maybe two years old. His name is Bobby."

She played nervously with the purse on her lap, opening and closing the clasp, adjusting the strap.

"I never even knew that she was pregnant."

DeKok leaned closer.

"Didn't you have *any* contact with her in the two years since you saw her last?" He sounded incredulous.

The old woman shrugged her shoulders reluctantly.

"Sometimes she wrote."

"Often?"

"The last letter was three months ago."

"And she didn't write about the child?"
"Not a word."

* * *

Vledder peeled back his sleeve and looked at his watch.

"It's about time. I'm going to the autopsy. Anything special you want?"

"Ask Dr, Rusteloos for a complete analysis of her blood, including blood-group, sub-groups, Rhesus factor, everything."

"Blood-group, but why?"

DeKok did not respond directly. He raked his fingers through his hair.

"I'll tell you later," he said absent-mindedly. "Also, be sure to ask about the murder weapon. Maybe he can give us a hint. And, of course, look for puncture marks."

"Puncture marks?"

"Yes," nodded DeKok, sounding tired, "I want to know *where* she injected herself. As far as I know, there wasn't a blemish on her arms."

Vledder pulled out his notebook and wrote importantly.

"Blood-group, sub-groups, weapon, puncture locations," he wrote. "That's all?"

DeKok ambled over to the coat rack and retrieved his ridiculous little hat.

"Give the doctor my best."

"What will you be doing?" Vledder wanted to know.

"I'm going to Emperor Street."

"Why?"

The gray sleuth smiled mysteriously.

"According to all the manuals, the killer often returns to the scene of the crime."

* * *

DeKok strolled leisurely down Warmoes Street and turned the corner toward Rear Fort Canal. He pushed his hat far back on his head and reflected that for once, he might have been cooler without it. He hesitated on the bridge across one of the canals. Only about a hundred yards away, on the corner of Barn Alley was the dimly lit, friendly establishment of Little Lowee, where he was wont to drink a glass of cognac and exchange the gossip of the Quarter with the mousey barkeeper. With a great deal of inner struggling, he overcame the temptation, considered that it was still early in the day and that Colette's murder had to take priority. He felt virtuous as he resolutely turned his back on visions of goldenbrown cognac in large, wafer-thin snifters.

He had nurtured hopes of developing the case in a sedate, routine atmosphere, to find the murderer in his familiar, calm tempo. In a quiet manner that was familiar to him and had so often led to success. DeKok did not believe in frenzied haste, armies of experts and legions of suspects. As he had remarked to Vledder not too long ago: According to a recent American study, eighty percent of all murder victims, *knew* their killers. DeKok had known that for years. Motive, means and opportunity were the crucial elements in any murder case. Find one and the other two would be discovered in due course. Find all three and it was just a matter of time before the killer was identified.

But the discovery of the child had disturbed the routine, had caused developments of which he could not yet foresee the consequences. He thought about Marianne Vanburen. The girl confused him. He wondered why that was ... why did she fascinate him so? There was something strange about her behavior ... something that attracted him and repulsed him at the same time.

He passed King Street and took a shortcut along Crooked Tree Ditch. The name had nothing to do with "crooked trees". In the old days, in the time of sail, it had been a channel for moving timber toward the shipyards. This particular channel had a bend in it, as opposed to Straight Tree Ditch, which used to be utilized in the same manner. In due course he approached the building at Emperor Street. He wondered if Ben Kruger and his cohorts had been able to find some usable prints.

Suddenly he stopped. A shadow moved behind the window on the second floor. The police had long since left. The small army of experts from the local station, augmented by specialists and technical people from Headquarters, would have left hours ago.

Carefully DeKok approached the front door of the soon to be demolished building. The door was open. Cautiously, step by step, willing the ancient treads to be silent, DeKok hoisted his two hundred pounds up the narrow stairs.

He stopped in the corridor at the top of the steps to catch his breath. Apparently he had not been heard. He listened intently. He heard a tearing sound from inside the room where the corpse had been found. It repeated several times. DeKok waited a few moments to get his breathing under control and then he kicked the door of the room. The door flew open and slammed against the wall.

Close to the window, bent over, was a man. Abruptly he straightened up and turned toward the noise. The long, dirty hair swept across his face.

DeKok observed every detail with photographic precision ... the wads of kapok from the ripped-open mattress, the jeans and the inevitable sneakers, an army jacket and a dagger, or long knife in the narrow hand.

Carelessly, a disarming smile on his lips, DeKok approached the man. Underneath the nonchalant pose, every fiber of his body was under tension because he saw fear and astonishment on the pale face before him.

Calmly, calculatingly, DeKok weighed the chances. He abhorred violence, never carried a weapon and was usually able to diffuse any situation. But the knife in the nervous hand was an obvious threat, a potential problem. Still smiling, he suddenly struck. With the suddenness of a striking cobra his hand closed around the wrist of the hand that held the knife. With an exclamation of pain, the young man released the weapon and DeKok kicked it into a far corner. His smile broadened.

"My name is DeKok," he said. It sounded like an apology. ". . . with kay-oh-kay," he clarified. He gave the man a friendly look and added: "Fred Mellenkamp, am I right?"

6

The astonishment slowly disappeared from his face. Some color returned to the pale cheeks of the young man. He pulled back his sleeve and looked at his wrist.

"You got damned hard hands," he said, rubbing the sore wrist.

DeKok looked at him for several long seconds.

"I'm never too pleased," he grinned finally, "when somebody stands in front of me with a bare blade. You could say I'm allergic to it. It always makes me itch."

The man readjusted his sleeve and raked a hand through his hair.

"I had no intention of hurting you."

DeKok gave him a winning smile.

"Surely you won't hold it against me," he said with light sarcasm. "You understand, in my profession . . . I'd rather be safe than sorry." He pointed at the ripped mattress. "What were you looking for?"

The young man pressed his lips together and shook his head.

"None of your business."

DeKok rubbed the bridge of his nose with a little finger.

"That's hardly an answer to my question. I'll be the judge of what is, or is not, my business. So . . . again: what were you looking for?"

The young man shook his head stubbornly.

"I won't tell you. I don't have to answer. I studied law, I know my rights."

DeKok nodded slowly and made a helpless gesture.

"In that case you are, I'm sure, aware of the rights of a simple police detective." He walked closer and placed a hand on the young man's shoulder. "Frederick Mellenkamp," he said in his official voice, "You're under arrest for the murder of Colette Maesen."

* * *

There was a suffocating atmosphere in the small interrogation room. Fred Mellenkamp jumped up and gestured violently. The long, dirty hair clung to his heated face in disorderly strands.

"It's stupid," he roared, "absolutely stupid. I didn't kill Colette Maesen. You're abrogating my liberty, it's unlawful detention. Your arrest has no basis in fact . . . you're lacking every possible legal ground."

DeKok abruptly leaned forward.

"Colette Maesen had something in her possession," he said sharply. "Something that you would like to have, want so badly you'd be prepared to kill for it . . . and did. When she didn't hand it over voluntarily, you beat in her brains and looked for it. But you couldn't find it in the room. Later, after her death, you realized she could have hidden it in the mattress. That's why you came back this afternoon and ripped it apart."

Mellenkamp shook his head in despair.

"A theory," he moaned, "a senseless theory." His blue eyes filled with tears. "It wasn't like that at all. Really, it wasn't like that." Then he fell back in his chair. "I didn't kill Colette."

DeKok grinned wickedly.

"I've never met a murderer who confessed during the first interrogation."

Mellenkamp jumped up again, angry and indignant.

"I'm not a murderer."

DeKok looked at him, expressionless.

"What were you looking for in the mattress?" he asked evenly.

Mellenkamp did not answer. He hid his face in his hands.

"It isn't important. It has nothing to do with her death."

DeKok's face remained expressionless, a hard mask.

"What were you looking for?" he repeated unperturbed.

The young man sighed. It was as if the relentless question on the same subject had undermined his strength, his willpower. He leaned forward and removed the hands from in front of his face.

"Heroin," he whispered. "Colette dealt in heroin. Some of her stash was left."

"How did you know?"

"I delivered it to her myself. Fifty grams. The day before she died. She had to have her stash somewhere."

"You're a user?"

Fred Mellenkamp shook his head slowly.

"Sometimes I have a customer."

"How long have you known Colette?"

"About as long as I know Marianne. I met them both near the monument on the Dam."

"Just like that?"

"What do you mean?'

"It was a coincidental meeting?"

"Yes. I was just enjoying the sun when they sat down next to me."

"And the child?"

"I saw him for the first time in Emperor Street. They had invited me over."

DeKok paused to observe the young man. The string of questions seemed to have calmed him down. The blue eyes were clear and the long, slender hands rested easily on the table top."

"You finished your law studies?"

"About two years ago."

"Why didn't you do something with it?"

That elicited a reaction of sorts. The hands moved, twitched nervously.

"I prefer the free life."

DeKok pushed his lower lip forward.

"A lot of people spent a lot of time and money to get you your education," he said sharply. "It's only fair that you make a contribution in return."

Mellenkamp reacted vehemently.

"What would you have me do?" he asked, despair and contempt in his voice. "I should sell myself for an astronomical salary to a bunch of executives of large corporations to point out legal ways for fleecing the public? Is that what you want?"

DeKok smiled faintly.

"You could offer legal assistance to people who have been falsely accused of murder."

Mellenkamp looked at him, a searching look in his eyes.

"You ... you're trying to tell me something?" he asked hesitantly.

The gray sleuth showed him a poker face.

"I don't believe you deal in heroin, not even sometimes and I also don't believe that's what you were looking for."

"Then what was I looking for?"

"If I knew that . . ." DeKok made an annoyed gesture. "If I knew that, Mr. Mellenkamp, then I would possibly also know who killed Colette." He rose slowly from his chair. "You may leave now."

The young man looked at him with surprise.

"I may leave?" he asked, astounded. "You're letting me go?"

DeKok nodded slowly. He invitingly held the door of the small interrogation room. The man rose. As he crossed the threshold, DeKok suddenly grabbed him by the lapels of his coat. Irresistibly, he brought the young man's face close to his own.

"If you," he hissed, "are responsible for Colette's death, no matter how . . . I'll find you, no matter where." He paused for effect. "With legal means, or without them."

The man swallowed. His adam's apple bobbed up and down.

"That," he said hoarsely, "is a threat."

DeKok grinned broadly.

"So it is, Mr. Mellenkamp," he said pleasantly, "so it is."

* * *

Robert Antoine Dijk, one of the younger Inspectors who had a bad case of hero-worship for DeKok looked a question at the old sleuth.

"What can I do for you?"

DeKok rubbed his eyes. He liked the young man but had no idea that Dijk worshipped him. Sometimes DeKok could be very obtuse.

"A mattress," he said listlessly. "A torn mattress. You'll find it in an abandoned building at Emperor Street, second floor. Use a car and take it to Dr. Eskes at the police lab. I'll call the good doctor ahead of time." He looked at the young man and examined the well-cut, dark-blue suit. He shook his head.

"You look a picture again," he said admiringly.

Dijk, much praised and teased for his fashionable clothes, ignored the remark.

"A mattress?" he asked.

DeKok gave him another close look.

"I'd wear a duster, or something," he said, concerned. "It's an old, dirty thing. A corpse rested on it for about three days and the stuffing is coming out."

The young inspector looked thoughtful.

"Is that connected with the killing of the homeless girl?"

"Indeed."

"Have you got any leads?"

"No . . . little."

"Could I . . . would you . . . may I?"

"Most certainly, my boy," said DeKok cheerfully. "I'd be glad of the help." He smiled. "Since you're going to the lab anyway . . . after you deliver the mattress, stop by at Headquarters and ask Chief-Inspector Everhard if he knows a certain Fred Mellenkamp. Everhard is with Narcotics . . . oh, you knew that? Very well, ask him about Mellenkamp. Supposedly Mellenkamp deals in heroin. No paperwork, you understand? Nothing official."

Dijk, who had been making notes, closed his notebook with a guilty look.

"Anything else?"

DeKok looked up at him.

"Robert, do you have children?"

"Yes, a girl of two and a boy of four."

"How old was your son when he started to talk?"

Dijk smiled shyly.

"About two, I think. He said a few words when he was just one and a half . . . you know, mama, papa, oma, hi, bye . . ."

"And now?"

A tender look showed on Dijk's face.

"He won't quit, a regular motor-mouth. He talks practically non-stop from the moment I get home, until he goes to bed."

"Does he talk about before?"

"Before?" Dijk seemed puzzled.

"Yes, does he ever talk about what happened before, before he could talk that well."

"His memories?" Dijk sounded skeptical.

"Exactly, Robert. Memories! Memories from the time he could hear, see and observe, but wasn't yet able to express his feelings in words."

"Why did you want to know?"

DeKok chewed his lower lip.

"You've heard about the case . . . the murdered girl . . . the child?"

"I read about it."

DeKok gestured.

"Suppose." he said pensively, "that the child was *not* in the closet when the killing happened . . . that he was a witness. If he is, you see, maybe he could tell us later what he had seen."

The young Inspector shrugged his shoulders. He looked doubtful.

"I'm not sure," he said, hesitantly, "if that's possible, if a child can talk about those things, anything, later. I never paid any attention to it in the case of my own son." He shook his head. "I don't think . . ."

DeKok waved the subject into oblivion.

"If they don't know Mellenkamp at Narcotics, check the central register."

Robert Antoine nodded his understanding. He turned around and left the detective room, an absorbed look in his eyes.

* * *

Sister Angelica lifted the little boy and proudly showed him off.

"Look at that," she said enthusiastically. "How does he look?"

"Magnificent," laughed DeKok.

She adjusted something on the sweater.

"We found a whole new outfit for Bobby, socks, shoes, everything."

"He's turning into the proper little gentleman," joked DeKok.

Sister Angelica stroked the child's cheek.

"He's still so pale, though," she said, concern in her voice. "It looks as if he hasn't been outside for months. We'll do a lot of walks with him." She bounced the child up and down on her knee. "He's going to be a *big* boy."

DeKok looked intently at the small boy, observed the blond hair, the blue eyes, the somewhat round face and he searched for a similarity.

"Have Colette's parents been?"

"They would have liked to have the child," nodded Sister Angelica. "Colette's sister and brother-in-law also showed interest. They have no children of their own. Of course, it will all be up to the Juvenile Protection Agency." Her tone of voice changed, became happier. "But for the time being . . . Bobby is going to stay with us."

DeKok rubbed the tip of his nose.

"Sister Angelica," he said diffidently, "You . . . eh, you spend a lot of time with Bobby?"

"I take care of him, yes."

"You talk with him?"

"A one-sided conversation," she laughed. "Bobby doesn't talk much . . . yet."

DeKok nodded his understanding.

"Would you mind," he went on, carefully, searching for words. "Would you mind doing something for me? . . . Nothing forced, you understand, as natural as possible . . . but talk to Bobby about what has happened. Maybe he'll say nothing, but a single word can be of the greatest importance to me."

She pulled a doubtful face.

"It would be better for Bobby if he forgot the past as soon as possible."

DeKok nodded smilingly. He leaned closer and stroked the child's hair.

"You're right, Sister," he said, dispirited. "Forget it. Maybe it's not all that important." He stood up and retrieved his little hat. Reluctantly he prepared to take his leave. "Bobby," he said wistfully, "used to have a little koala . . ."

7

Lowee the barkeeper was, because of his spare stature, commonly referred to as "Little" Lowee. He was also, not coincidentally, DeKok's friend and primary informer. Lowee was a crook of the old school who considered himself several steps above the modern gangsters and drug traffickers. He dealt in booze, women, stolen boodle and as a clearing house for underworld gossip.

When he saw DeKok appear in the door opening of his establishment, he hastily wiped his hands on an apron and stretched out his hand across the bar.

"I ain't seen you for some time," he chirped.

The gray sleuth hoisted himself on a barstool.

"Business before pleasure," he grunted.

"Business before cognac?" queried the barkeeper with a twinkle in his eye. He dived underneath the counter and emerged with a bottle of magnificent cognac. With the same, routine gesture he placed two large snifters on the counter. He held up the bottle to enable DeKok to admire the label. "Same recipe?"

Without waiting for an answer he poured the golden liquid in the waiting glasses. He put down the bottle and the crook and the cop lifted their glasses toward each other, carefully cradling the fragile glass in the hollow of their hands. Then, as if by silent agreement, they simultaneously lifted the glasses to their lips for the first, careful sip. It was a ceremony that belonged as much to DeKok as his badge. He and Lowee had known each other from the time that DeKok was still a uniformed constable and had to sneak into Lowee's bar when the opportunity presented itself. These days he visited Lowee' place at least three, sometimes four times a week.

Lowee put down his glass.

"I hear you took the kid from them two chippies. Black Josie tole me. Her and Rika done seen you at the station, ain't it?"

"I didn't take the child away," denied DeKok. "One of the girls has been murdered in that abandoned building they were using. I found the child in a hall closet."

The small barkeeper made "tut-tut" sounds.

"Poor kid. All the working girls said it was a bummer. You knows them, DeKok, ain't gotta tell you. Some of them was gonna tell you weeks ago."

"What?"

"Well, you knows . . . about the kid and them peddling it."

DeKok took another sip.

"I wish they had." He stared into the distance. "Maybe the girl would still be alive today.

"Why were she killed?"

DeKok grinned ruefully.

"I've been pondering that for more than twenty-four hours."

"You thinks the kid got somewhat to do with it?"

"With what?"

"With the murder, of course."

DeKok cocked his head at the small barkeeper.

"How's that again?" he asked.

Little Lowee did not answer at once. He licked his lips and darted a hunted look around the bar. Only Vledder and DeKok knew that he sometimes supplied information to the old cop and he would like to keep it that way.

"They ain't offered the kid around here alone, you knows," he whispered. "Had a geezer in the bar, right here, that were innerested too."

"When?"

"About three days ago."

"What sort of man?"

"Justa guy." Lowee shrugged his shoulders. "I mean, nuthin special . . . well dressed, I give you that. Gray suit, hat and scarf. Looked like one of them guvvement johnnies, you knows. Real la-di-da voice, you know like they swallowered a frog."

"How old?"

"Forty . . . maybe forty-five. Grayish onna side."

"Where did he come from?"

"Who knows. I ain't asked."

"Did he ask for Bobby?"

Little Lowee shook his head.

"Nah, he asked for a young woman anna kid."

"A vague description, don't you think?"

The small barkeeper leaned closer and whispered in a confidential tone.

"I knowed he was gonna come."

"You knew?"

"Yessir," nodded Lowee. "A few days before one of them gals shows up here and asks iffen I wanna sent a guy over to that building. She tole me what the geezer will ask."

"So, the man was expected."

"Yessir, you betcha. They tole him to come here for directions."

"And what was in it for you?"

"Me . . . what for?"

"For your . . . eh, to act as go-between . . ."

"Nuthin!" Lowee shook his head indignantly. "Ain't no sweat offa my back."

"Just a friendly gesture?"

"Yep . . . you coulda say so."

DeKok nodded his understanding. He searched an inner pocket and withdrew a photograph, one of the close-ups made by Weelen.

"This girl?"

Lowee took the picture and studied it.

"Yessir," he said decidedly, "it were her. She done ask me." He looked up at Dekok. "They killed her?"

"Colette Maesen," nodded DeKok.

"They woulda been better off to take the other, the one with the black hair." He shook his head pityingly.

The remark surprised DeKok.

"Why do you say that?"

The small barkeeper gestured vaguely, a glass in his hand.

"The other ain't no good, believe you me. A serpent if ever there were one. The same type as me old lady, me mother. When she put us to bed at night, you'd think 'whatta angel' and two minutes later she'd be tearing my old man another as. . . another . . . she'd yell at him," he concluded lamely. Even Lowee knew DeKok's opinion about strong language and avoided it whenever possible. It was the sort of thing you did for a friend, even if he was a cop.

DeKok laughed heartily. He lifted his glass and took another sip. Lowee always poured generous measures.

"So you sent the guy to Emperor Street?"

"Yep."

"What time was that?"

"Three, maybe four in the afternoon."

"Did you talk to him at all, before that."

"Not so as you'd notice. He ordered port and asks iffen I seen the child. So I says yes, because I *done* seen 'em when those two was peddling 'im. They came in here too."

DeKok rubbed the bridge of his nose with a little finger.

"So the man came especially for the child," he re-emphasized. "I mean, he didn't come for the girl, either girl. You know they sometimes took clients."

"Nah, for the kid," assured Lowee. His friendly, mousey face was expressionless. "Tha's what I thinks. The geezer was full of it. He took out his wallet and showed me a picture."

"A picture of the child?

"Of the kid," confirmed Lowee calmly.

DeKok swallowed with amazement.

"Pour me another one," he said, perplexed.

Little Lowee obeyed with the speed and grace of a good publican.

* * *

Vledder listened intently to DeKok's report of what had happened. His eyes flashed and his face was red.

"*That's* the killer," he exclaimed. "*That's* the guy who must have done it. It's almost a foregone conclusion. I mean, the time, everything, it all fits . . . it computes. Three days ago he was at Lowee's . . . Lowee sent him to Emperor Street . . . between three and four . . . almost exactly the time of death . . ."

"It *could* have happened that way," agreed DeKok.

Vledder gestured wildly.

"We'll have to comb the neighborhood . . . find witnesses. *Somebody* must have seen him."

"Where?"

"On Emperor Street, near the building. Now that we have a description, we should try it."

"Then what?"

"What do you mean?"

"Let's suppose we find a witness who saw the man there, that afternoon. Then what? How did you want to find him?" He grinned. "How many well-dressed men between forty and forty-five do you think there are?"

Vledder shrugged his shoulders.

"As you so often say yourself, we're cops." He paused. Then continued enthusiastically. "But don't you see? There's a connection. There's a thread somewhere. All we have to do is follow the thread. Eventually we'll reach him."

DeKok stood up and started to pace up and down the detective room. He did that often to help organize his thoughts. It was the next best thing to walking the streets of his beloved Amsterdam. He stopped in front of Vledder's desk.

"Colette," he said pensively, "had the man come to Lowee's bar. I made sure when I questioned Lowee. The man did *not* come for Colette, but because he *knew* that Colette had a blond child."

Vledder suddenly clapped his hands to his mouth.

"I . . . eh, I forgot to tell you something," he stammered, abashed and confused. "I'm sorry . . . it's about the autopsy."

"Well?"

"A remark by Dr. Rusteloos about the child."

It was DeKok's turn to look confused.

"What's the matter with the child?"

Vledder swallowed.

"It isn't hers, Colette's child, I mean. It *couldn't* be Colette's. Colette has never been pregnant."

8

Detective-Inspector DeKok walked around his desk and sat down behind it.

"Colette has never been pregnant," he said tonelessly, repeating it to himself. He looked at his younger colleague. "Did he say anything special about it?"

"No, I was under the impression that it was easy to establish. As usual, I had a short conversation with Dr. Rusteloos *before* the autopsy. The way we found the corpse, where and so on. I also told him about the child we found in the closet." The young Inspector made a helpless gesture. "You know how he is ... don't bother him while he's working. He just cuts away and whispers into that little microphone of his. About half-way through the autopsy he says, apropos of nothing, that she has never been pregnant. I asked him to repeat it and he did. I was too surprised to ask any further questions. It's a bit silly that I forgot all about it until you mentioned the child and ..." He did not complete the sentence, but made an apologetic gesture. "Sorry, DeKok, I ... eh, I ..."

DeKok indulgently waved away all excuses.

"I understand," he said philosophically. "In a matter of speaking it's my own fault. I should have asked you to ask Dr.

Rusteloos about it. I should have asked how long ago she had delivered a baby, if that can be determined at all."

"But why?" asked Vledder, taken aback. "Surely that was never a question? As far as I know, we never doubted that Bobby was Colette's child."

DeKok did not answer at once. He placed his elbows on the edge of the desk and rested his chin on his folded hands.

"I had some doubts," he said at last. "For instance, her severe degree of addiction. It seldom happens to mother's with small children . . . at least here in Holland. And if she was that much addicted, why would anybody trust her to be a dealer? That hasn't been answered yet, by the way. In any case, the possibilities existed. I had to take them into account. Then, when her parents told me they never even knew she had a child, my suspicion grew. That's why I asked for a complete breakdown, a minute classification, of her blood."

Vledder's eyes widened.

"Of course, you wanted to compare it with the child's blood."

"Just to be sure," nodded DeKok. "I wanted to eliminate every possible doubt."

"Well, that has happened," commented Vledder. "Maybe not the way you suspected, but Dr. Rusteloos has answered the question conclusively."

DeKok pushed back his chair.

"To be replaced by another question . . . if the child is not Colette's, how did she get the child?"

Vledder had an answer for that.

"Stolen," he suggested promptly.

DeKok looked pensive.

"I wouldn't be so sure about that," he pondered. "You have to keep in mind that Colette had the child for some time. She already had the child when Marianne met her, sometime in May.

And as far as I know, there have been no reports regarding missing children of about that age, during that period. We would have known. Crimes against children are taken very seriously."

"Maybe she had custody of the child . . . on a temporary basis . . . a sort of baby-sitting?"

DeKok raked stubby fingers through his hair.

"But who would entrust a child to an addict?"

"Another addict?"

DeKok bit his lower lip and shook his head.

"Colette Maesen acted as if Bobby was her own child. Just think about the prostitutes she approached and the man who came to Lowee's to . . ." He stopped suddenly. Quickly he rose from his chair and walked over to the coat rack.

Vledder followed him with his eyes.

"Where are you going?"

DeKok placed his old felt hat on his head and turned toward his partner.

"Marianne," he said curtly, "I want to know what *she* knows about that meeting."

Vledder followed hastily.

* * *

"Everything." Marianne Vanburen swept her long hair from in front of her face. "I knew all about the plan. I was the one who advised her. In fact, it was *my* plan to have that guy come to Amsterdam."

"To the bar? Lowee's place?"

"That seemed the best way. In any case, it seemed better than to give him the address in Emperor Street. We didn't want him to be able to check things out."

"Why not?"

She shrugged her shoulders.

"An abandoned building," she said reluctantly. "We were afraid he wouldn't show up if he knew."

"But he came?"

"I presume so." She gestured vaguely. "Otherwise Colette wouldn't have died."

"Wouldn't have died?" repeated DeKok while his eyebrows rippled across his forehead. It was the second time Marianne had observed the phenomenon and again she seemed spellbound. DeKok had to repeat his question, but not until his eyebrows had come to rest, did she answer.

She looked at him angrily, shaking her head.

"Colette didn't want me to be there. She wanted to meet him by herself. It was private business, she said and she sent me away to do some shopping. That's also why I was never allowed to see the letter she sent him."

"So . . . you've never met him?"

"No."

"And you don't know who he is . . . where he lives?"

"No," she sighed, exasperated. "I only know that he exists, that's all." She cocked her head at DeKok, a coquettish look in her eyes. "If I knew more about him, I would have told you long ago. I want Colette's killer caught as much as you."

The Inspector looked back at her and again was overcome by a feeling of confusion.

"Why did Colette ask him to come?"

"For the money," she smiled without joy. "After all, it was ridiculous that we had to live in a target for the wrecker's ball while that guy stank with money."

"But why," asked DeKok, grinning sheepishly, "would he pay you?"

"He's Bobby's father," she said, tossing her head.

DeKok smiled thinly.

"Bobby has no father," he said. "Not Bobby, Bobby only has a procreator," he concluded with a fair imitation of the girl's voice.

The sarcasm seemed to confuse her momentarily. Then she recovered.

"That's right," she said sharply.

"And the man?"

She closed her eyes, amazed at so much incomprehension.

"We made him believe he was the father," she explained patiently, as if it should have been obvious. "Colette said she had dated him several times. He was a rich guy, millions, according to Colette." She paused, twirled her hair around her fingers. "I asked if she had gone to bed with him."

"And when Colette admitted that, you were ready with a little blackmail scheme," said DeKok grimly.

Marianne lowered her head, her fingers plucked nervously at her skirt. One breast almost, but not quite, escaped from the confines of her open blouse.

"I said," she whispered, "I said ... eh, ... send him Bobby's picture and ask if he's got something left over."

"While you knew the man was married?"

"Yes."

"As I said ... blackmail."

She jumped up out of her chair, eyes flashing.

"Yes," she screamed, loud and wild, "blackmail! And why not? The whole world is held together with blackmail, intrigue and cheating. How did you think that geezer gathered his millions? With honest work?"

DeKok rubbed the bridge of his nose with a little finger.

"You're bitter," he concluded somberly. "You should try to approach life more positively. Don't always look for the negative, especially when you're looking in a mirror."

He flicked his eyes at Vledder who, in response to the unspoken request, gently urged her back into her chair.

"So," resumed DeKok when she was again seated, "Colette sent Bobby's picture to this unknown man?"

"I presume so. I never saw it."

"Where did Colette have the picture taken?"

"I think she already had it." He tone was surly, accompanied by a nonchalant shrugging of the shoulders.

"And the koala?"

"That too." For just an instance a tender look fled across her face. "Bobby always played with it. He was crazy about that little toy. He would clutch it in his arms when he went to sleep."

"Did Colette ever tell you anything about the time before she met you? I mean . . . was it a difficult delivery . . . did she breastfeed Bobby?"

Marianne Vanburen shook her head, casting a suspicious glance in his direction.

"No . . . no, she never talked about that."

DeKok gave her a winning, reassuring smile. He leaned forward, shortening the distance between them.

"Then again," he said, "that would have been difficult, don't you think? He wasn't Colette's child at all, you see. Colette has never even been pregnant."

The expression on her face changed.

"N-never b-been p-pregnant?" she stuttered, shocked and scared. Her lower lip quivered. DeKok observed her dispassionately.

"It was discovered when they cut her open," he said brutally.

Suddenly she looked pale, all color drained from her face and the blue eyes turned up, glazed over. Slowly she slid sideways off the chair. Vledder rushed over but was just a split second late. Before he could reach her, she collapsed unconscious on the floor.

9

Vledder was slightly irritated with his old mentor.

"Did you have to? Was there no other way?"

DeKok stared gloomily out of the window. He felt depressed and melancholy. The case was not to his liking, was not developing as he wanted. His worries were not just for the murder of Colette, but also, to a great extend for the girl Marianne. He wondered if it would not be better to withdraw from the case, turn it over to someone else. Was he losing his objectivity? The strange girl influenced his thinking, awakened feelings in him he found hard to suppress. It made him unsure of himself.

"Did you have to do that?" repeated Vledder, louder.

DeKok turned around, his thoughts still far away.

"You're right," he said tiredly. "It could have been done differently. More friendly, less shocking." He paused, rubbed his eyes. "How is she now?"

"Major Bossart is taking care of her personally. She took her away and put her to bed."

"Did the Major say anything?"

Vledder smiled bitterly.

"She said that you should have more understanding for the girl. That we shouldn't forget that Marianne has lived under considerable stress for some time. The death of Colette has shocked her deeply. She has no one left now . . . no friend, no Bobby."

DeKok pressed his lips together, swallowed.

"I *do* understand," he said after a while, his tone was harsh. "Believe me, by now I'm pretty well aware of what goes on in her mind. But just understanding . . . sympathy, if you will . . . doesn't solve a murder." He raised a finger in the air. "Let's be honest with each other. If the two young ladies conspired to commit blackmail and one of them is presented with an accounting, then it's sad, certainly not to be excused, but . . . it's understandable."

Vledder straddled a chair backward, resting his arms on the backrest.

"How're we going to find the guy?"

DeKok looked down on him from his standing position.

"You said it already . . . follow the thread. I think the most important thing is that the man responded to the invitation. He didn't ignore it, but rushed right over to Lowee's place. That means that there must have been a relationship, and I emphasize *relationship*, that *could* have resulted in a child. And the man knew that. If we start digging into Colette's past, we have to find him."

Vledder frowned.

"How was that again? A neat, well-dressed man with a cultured voice, between forty and forty five, slightly graying at the temples."

"More or less exactly Lowee's words," smiled DeKok.

* * *

They walked through Old Bridge Alley toward the Damrak and from there to the New Dike. A barrel organ played on the corner of Whirlpool Alley and DeKok slowed his pace to enjoy the music as long as possible. He nodded at the man with the cap and tossed the traditional quarter in his direction. The man used the cap to catch it in mid-air, without spilling any of the other quarters in the cap. He would have been a mean racquet ball player, thought Vledder as he watched the man knuckle his forehead in thanks. Then he grinned to himself. Imagine being beaten by a tobacco chewing octogenarian with a peg leg.

Soon they reached Saint Jacob Street and stopped in front of 112. It was a small, old two-story house with high windows and a decorative neck roof. The hard-green front door was ajar.

DeKok pushed back his sleeve and looked at his watch. Just eleven in the morning, he thought, a good time to visit an artist in his studio.

They climbed the narrow stairs and knocked on the door on the second floor. It sounded hollow and empty and was without results. DeKok knocked again, harder and louder. Again no reaction. Everything remained quiet, except for the distant dripping of a tap, somewhere in the house. Vledder tried the doorknob and when it gave, he pushed open the door. They found themselves in a long, narrow room with a stained hard-wood floor. Immediately to the right of the door was an old-fashioned clothes press. To the left, in the corner, they saw a brass bed. Slowly they approached the bed. A tuft of blonde hair peeked out from beneath a gray blanket.

DeKok coughed demonstratively. There was some movement under the gray blanket. Suddenly, she sat up straight. A stunning girl with long blonde hair that cascaded in waves to below her shoulder. DeKok heard a panting grunt from Vledder next to him.

DeKok looked at her searchingly. He estimated her to be in her early twenties. As far as could be seen, she wore no clothing and made no effort to cover herself. She looked at the two men with a set of bright green eyes and just a hint of surprise.

"Who are you?" she asked with a hoarse, sensuous voice.

DeKok hesitated for a moment, then he gave her his best smile.

"My name is DeKok ... with kay-oh-kay." He pointed a thumb at Vledder. "This is Vledder. We're police inspectors."

She wrinkled her nose and pushed out her chin. Her perfect breasts bobbed pleasantly as she shrugged her shoulders.

"Cops ... what do you want?"

DeKok swallowed. His puritanical soul rebelled at the sight of the naked young woman. The aesthetic part of his being admired her and silently wished her to maintain the pose indefinitely.

"We ... we're looking for Karel Karsemeyer."

She looked at the empty spot in the bed.

"He isn't here," she concluded simply. "As you can see. He's probably taking care of breakfast."

"You ... the two of you live together?"

She chuckled naughtily, leaning back on her arms, confusing both men with the sight of her luscious body. The laughter seemed to start deep in her taut belly and rippled up from there. Her entire body seemed to laugh.

"Well, it looks that way, don't you think?"

Vledder grinned enviously, but Dekok remained unperturbed. He again had himself under control.

"How long?" asked DeKok.

"What do you mean?"

"How long have you been living together?"

She shrugged with a perfect left shoulder, apparently unaware of what it did to the rest of her body and the effect it had on the average healthy male.

"One and a half, maybe two years or thereabouts. I don't know exactly. I'll ask Karel. He'll be able to tell you." She pointed at a bench against the wall. "Have a seat. I guess he went for bread and butter. We were out."

Stark naked she emerged from between the blankets and pulled a camisole over her head. The lacy garment was transparent, with a deep decollete and hardly reached below her waist. She leaned forward, affording a view of a perfectly round behind and picked up a pair of jeans from the floor. As she stepped into to them, balancing on one leg, she asked:

"What's up. Why do you need Karel?"

The gray sleuth gestured vaguely, glancing away from the reverse strip-tease.

"We just want to talk to him."

Thankfully, thought DeKok, she slipped into a blouse that went over the provocative undergarment. While she buttoned her blouse, she pointed her head at a collection of paintings on the wall.

"Karel paints old masters." She laughed infectiously. "He paints just like the old masters," she corrected cheerfully. "He's very good at it." She sat down across from the cops and threw one leg over the other. "Sometimes people feel cheated."

"We're not here for that," said DeKok, shaking his head. He rubbed the bridge of his nose and changed the subject. "Do you know Colette Maesen?"

"Who's that?"

"She used to live here."

"With Karel?"

"That's what I heard," said DeKok diffidently.

A pensive look came into the green eyes. Her beautiful face became introspective.

"Was it a girl from Utrecht?"

"Yes," nodded DeKok, "Colette Maesen was from Utrecht."

The girl scratched her head, thinking.

"She was an addict, I seem to remember. Karel told me about her."

She rose and walked over to a stack of paintings against the wall. With quick movements she flipped through the unframed paintings and then pulled one of them out. With a tender gesture she placed it against a chair. The light from the high windows caressed the colors. It was a dreamy, almost ethereal painting. Colette's face emerged hazily from mild, sweet ochers. The girl looked down on the painting.

"Karel never wanted to get rid of it," she said softly.

A big, heavy man thundered into the room. He carried a paper bag in one mighty arm. DeKok looked at him and recognized him at once from the photo Colette's mother had shown him. The girl walked to meet him.

"Two gentlemen from the constabulary." She pointed at the painting. "They're here because of her."

The man placed the paper bag on the floor and concentrated his attention toward DeKok.

"What's the matter with Colette?" he asked in a deep, rumbling base.

DeKok ignored the question.

"When did she leave you?" he asked.

"Two years ago." The man stared at the painting. "Shortly before Pauline came."

DeKok pointed at the girl.

"Pauline?"

The man nodded with a smile.

"Colette didn't want to stay any longer. She *had* to leave, she said, she thought she could manage." He sat down on the edge of the bed. "I found her . . .. at night, in the streets. She was literally in the gutter . . . a total loss."

"When?"

"About three years ago." He gestured vaguely. "She was with me for at least a year. In bad shape when I found her. Addicted . . . crack. Nasty shit. Not easy to kick." The man spoke in short, staccato sentences, as if giving instructions to a model. "She was dirty," he went on. "Filthy, neglected. She stank. Rags on her body. I washed her. Gave her one of my shirts. Next morning I took her in hand. Live or die, I told her . . . your choice. She chose for Life. OK, I said, but no more shit."

"Did she stick to it?"

He laughed heartily, showing a row of strong, white, healthy teeth.

"Didn't have a chance. Couldn't get it. I watched her like a hawk. Never alone. She cursed me, swore at me. Fought me. Took six months before she became human again . . . more or less." He left unclear if the transformation was more or less successful, or if the time was more or less six months. He paused, rubbed his hands together. "You can't keep a person prisoner. Never works out. A person is born to be free. I just helped her, supported her, as long as necessary. When she wanted to leave . . . and I thought she could, I held the door for her."

"With bleeding heart?"

Karel Karsemeyer looked at DeKok. His brown eyes were moist and his large hands rhythmically rubbed his knees.

"Why should I deny it? It hurt me. I had been with her so long . . . watched over her so long. Almost day and night, in the beginning. She was part of my life."

DeKok nodded his understanding and remained silent. After a long pause he finally spoke.

"Yesterday I talked to her parents," he said. "They were very pleased with you. Full of praise. They still keep your photo."

Karel Karsemeyer stroked his magnificent beard, a playful smile around his lips.

"They've been here. He was an engineer with the Railways. A fine old gentleman ... full of understanding." He shook his head solemnly. "Not her. The mother wasn't so fine. I think it was *her* fault that Colette ..." Suddenly he stopped, looked again at the old cop. It was as if he suddenly realized who he was talking to. A suspicious look came into his eyes.

"Why are you here? Did something happen to Colette?"

DeKok hesitated, scratched the back of his neck.

"Two days ago," he said hesitantly, "we found her in an old abandoned building."

The man's face froze.

"How?"

The gray sleuth shook his head sadly.

"She could no longer be saved."

The man stared at him. It took a while before the meaning of DeKok's words penetrated. Then he clapped both hands in front of his face and started to sob.

"Colette ... Colette."

It sounded so heart-breaking, so sad and sorrowful that DeKok felt a lump in his throat. He stood up. Vledder followed suit.

The man took away his hands from his face and looked up with a teary face.

"When is she being buried?"

"Tomorrow at ten. At Sorrow Field."

"May I come?"

DeKok swallowed with difficulty.

"Colette would have wanted that," he said kindly.

10

"There was no heroin in the mattress. They checked it thoroughly." Robert Antoine Dijk looked disappointed. "There never was any heroin in it, as far as they could tell."

"The needle . . . have they checked the hypodermic yet?"

"According to Dr. Eskes," nodded Dijk, "his report on that went out at the same time as the report on the wallet."

"And?"

"It was used for heroin."

"I see." DeKok flipped through some pages of the autopsy report. "She used the indirect method. Colette did not inject into the vein, but used her upper thigh."

"What does that mean?"

"It makes little difference," answered DeKok. "It just takes a little longer before the drug takes effect. Most addicts won't wait for that. They want instant gratification." He pushed the report aside. "And how was Fred Mellenkamp?"

Robert Antoine shook his head.

"He's not in our records. At Narcotics they had also never heard of him. I checked Central Files, but he was unknown in The Hague* as well."

---

* Although Amsterdam is the constitutional Capital of the Netherlands, the seat of government, the senate, house of representatives, the cabinet and all cabinet departments are located in The Hague. In effect the Netherlands have *two* capital cities.

DeKok grinned without mirth.

"A *nice* boy . . . no police record."

"They all start that way," grinned Dijk cynically. "With a virgin police record, I mean." He stood up. "Is there anything else I can do for you?"

DeKok nodded slowly.

"Keep digging into Mellenkamp's background. Apparently he studied Law, graduated, but never took his Bar exams."

Vledder came over as soon as Dijk had left. He crossed his arms and pushed out his chin. His stance was a bit arrogant, self-conscious and challenging.

DeKok looked up to him from his chair and gazed at him with surprise.

"What's the matter with you?" he asked gruffly.

"What are we working on?" asked Vledder.

DeKok looked mystified.

"The murder of Colette Maesen."

"Excellent," said Vledder sarcastically, "really excellent. "And why did we go to Karel Karsemeyer?"

DeKok smiled. Indulgently he joined in the game.

"In order to find out about Colette's past."

Vledder nodded emphatically.

"Right. To find the man who visited her on the day of her death. Remember? Forty something, gray at the temples?"

DeKok gestured toward the chair next to his desk.

"Sit down," he said calmly. "I get a crick in my neck from looking up at you."

The young Inspector sat down reluctantly.

"You never talked about that man," accused the younger partner. "You didn't mention him to Pauline, nor that painter. Not so much as a hint. Not a single question in that direction. I also didn't hear you say anything about the child."

DeKok did not react at once. A sad look came over his face as he gazed for long seconds at his assistant. He liked his young friend and did not want to hurt him.

"If," he began carefully, "this morning in Saint Jacob Street you hadn't been so much impressed by the shapely Pauline . . . you might have followed the conversation more closely and thought about it . . . Maybe you would not be making unfounded accusations." He paused and smiled broadly. "Perhaps you would have come to a certain conclusion."

Vledder looked puzzled. He knew his old mentor well and he knew that DeKok was telling him, as gently as possible, that he might have been precipitous.

"Conclusion?" he asked, unsure of himself.

DeKok nodded, but before he could answer, he was interrupted by the telephone. The gray sleuth lifted the receiver and listened. The amicable expression on his face changed. The lines hardened.

"I'll be there," he said curtly and hung up.

Vledder looked at him tensely.

"What's up?"

DeKok stood up. His mouth was a thin, straight line. His face was pale.

"Bobby's disappeared."

* * *

The small nun, Sister Angelica, looked up at him with a teary face.

"I couldn't help it," she sobbed, shaking her head. "Really, I couldn't."

DeKok sat down next to her and placed a protective arm around her shoulders.

"Of course you couldn't help it. Nobody's blaming you."

She calmed down. The sobbing subsided.

"They stole him."

"Who?"

"I don't know." She wiped the back of her hand over her eyes. "It was nice weather this afternoon. Sunny. I thought, I'll take Bobby out, I'm going to take him for a walk. The child needed fresh air. Usually I don't have that much spare time, but this afternoon I did." She gestured. "Here, in the inner city, there's nothing, no greenery . . . just cars and stink. So I took him to Nassau Square and took the bus to Wester Park. There's a large meadow in the center of the park. Some old men on benches and a lot of mothers with children. I sat down on a bench and allowed Bobby to play in the grass."

"What time was that?"

"About two, half past."

"Then what?"

"Of course, I watched him." Sister Angelica swallowed. "As best as I could. A woman came to sit next to me, about thirty, I think. She had a baby with her in a pram. The woman started to talk to me, about herself, the baby, her husband . . . and that she used to be Catholic." Sister Angelica adjusted her habit. "The woman was very open. She needed to talk. I felt that and I didn't want to disappoint her. There's so much loneliness. Eventually I started to preach, or rather, it was more a . . ." She stopped, started to sob again. "Suddenly he was gone. Just gone. He was no longer with the other children in the grass. I called, searched, asked everybody if they had seen Bobby. I was in a panic, I ran all across the park." A handkerchief appeared magically in her hands and she dried her eyes. "They took him away. There's no other explanation. He could never have gotten that far on his own." She looked at him. "You understand? He can barely walk."

DeKok scratched the tip of his nose.

"How long were you talking?"

"That's hard to say." She shrugged her shoulders. "Half an hour, forty-five minutes. The woman had a lot to say."

DeKok nodded to himself.

"Did you see a girl in a multi-colored skirt with long, black hair?"

Sister Angelica shook her head sadly.

"I didn't notice."

DeKok insisted.

"Perhaps in the bus. Somebody must have followed you."

Again she shook her head.

"Bus Twelve was full," she said. "There were no seats left. Somebody offered me his seat and I took Bobby on my lap. Perhaps a girl like that was on the bus ... I didn't pay any attention."

DeKok rose.

"Don't worry about it," he said encouragingly. "We'll find Bobby." He patted her shoulder and walked away. Near the door he turned around and gave her a confident smile. In his heart he wondered anxiously if he could keep his promise.

* * *

"What next?"

DeKok growled in reply. His face was grave.

"Stupid we didn't make pictures of the child at once. Our job would be a lot easier."

Vledder looked at him with surprise.

"Why stupid? Surely, we could not be expected to know that the child would be stolen?"

DeKok slammed his fist on the desk. The disappearance of the child worried him, increased his feeling of uneasiness, the feeling of guilt.

"It should never have happened," he burst out bitterly. "I should have foreseen it. Right from the start, Bobby should have been better guarded, protected. Heroin is not the root cause of this case at all. It's the child! Colette was killed because of the child."

Vledder spread both arms.

"But why?" he asked theatrically. "Who wants the child so badly that he's willing to kill for it?" He shook his head in despair. "What does that get us? Where are you going to hide afterwards? The child would be an encumbrance, you can't hide it forever. Someday you have to come out into the open."

DeKok scratched the back of his neck.

"But that can take months, maybe years. We have to find Bobby as soon as possible. That's important for the child, as well as for us. Is the APB out?"

"Yes," nodded Vledder. "The whole country has been alerted, including the border crossings. And . . . I informed Interpol."

DeKok stared into the distance.

"Work up something for the press," he said finally. "Nothing specific, nothing about the background. Just something to the effect that a child has disappeared from Wester Park . . . as complete a description as possible . . . offer a reward. You know what I mean." He looked at the large clock on the wall and noted it was almost five o'clock. "Too late for the evening papers," he thought out loud. "And I'll never get permission for using radio and TV, not yet, anyway. The case is still too fresh."

Vledder made some notes and switched on his computer screen. The door of the detective room opened and two nuns entered. They were directed toward DeKok's desk. Sister Angelica walked in front, followed by a shy nun with a sweet face. DeKok had never seen her. He stood up to greet them. Sister Angelica was still pale.

"This is Sister Maria," she said. "I asked her to come. We're all very much upset about Bobby's disappearance. We hardly talk about anything else. I said rather emphatically that Bobby has been stolen, but, of course, I don't know for sure. It could be an accident. There's water in the park and close by. Maybe he fell in the water. It's so easy to say *the child has been stolen* and blame someone else."

DeKok smiled at her.

"Don't torture yourself so," he admonished.

She suppressed a new wave of tears with considerable effort.

"We want to do anything possible to help you find Bobby." She pointed at the second nun. "Sister Maria took a picture of Bobby . . . yesterday, during a small party for Sister Francisca. The film is still in the camera. We hope it comes out."

Sister Maria handed DeKok a simple camera.

"There are a few pictures left," she explained. "Three I think . . . but it doesn't matter."

DeKok handed the camera to Vledder.

"We're very glad to have it," he said. "We'll have it developed and printed at once."

Both nuns stood up and took their leave. Halfway to the door, Sister Angelica turned around and came toward the desk. DeKok rose courteously, a question on his face.

"You . . . eh, you asked me to talk to Bobby about . . . before, about things that happened earlier?"

"Yes."

She nodded over her shoulder, in the direction of Sister Maria.

"Bobby . . . Bobby had a word he kept repeating."

"What word?" prompted DeKok.

She leaned closer.

"Bobo."

11

Little Lowee showed a comical look on his friendly, mousy face.

"The women is full of it," he exclaimed. "Them rumors won't quit. The whole Quarter is buzzing like a hornest nest."

"What about?"

"The child." The small barkeeper leaned forward on the bar. "They say it's the kid offa Eyetalian guest worker, who wanted to take it with 'em to his family in Italy. The Dutch mother was besides herself and inna attack of craziness gave it to some homeless broads."

"Nonsense."

"But it's wha they says, all over the streets." He gestured violently, his tone was hurt.

DeKok sipped from his glass of a cognac, a stubborn look on his face.

"Sensation, nothing but sensation," he grunted.

The diminutive barkeeper shrugged his shoulders.

"But it *coulda* be that way," he persisted, offended. "You read it alla time in the papers."

DeKok replaced his glass on the bar.

"Anything is possible," he growled. "I hear we even put a man on the moon."

"We done?" asked Lowee, momentarily distracted. "I thought it were them Yanks."

"Last time I heard," said DeKok in an irritated tone of voice, "The Americans were just as human as the rest of us."

Lowee looked at him carefully.

"Something bothering you?" he asked. "You don't sound like yourself at all, nossir, you doesn't."

DeKok rubbed his face.

"They stole the child," he said brusquely, an indifferent look on his face that did not fool the small man behind the bar. "In Wester Park. I had taken it to the Sisters for the time being. This afternoon one of them allowed the child to play in the park and suddenly he was gone."

Lowee's little, beady eyes opened wide.

"That geezer did it," he asserted suddenly. "Betcha dollars to donuts, that guy and a woman."

The gray sleuth looked up in surprise.

"What guy? What woman?"

Lowee gestured expansively.

"The geezer, I tole you about 'im . . . the one with the gray on the side of his head. He was here again, this afternoon. With a woman."

"In the bar?"

"No, not in here." Lowee shook his head. "In the neighborhood."

"Did you see him?"

"Not me . . . Old Karl."

DeKok narrowed his eyes.

"How did Old Karl know the man?" he asked suspiciously.

"Old Karl was here," nodded Lowee, "the day the guy come for the first time and axed about the kid. He was sitting right there, atta end of the bar, his regular spot. When the geezer paid and was gonna leave, Old Karl said something like he coulda have bought a round." Lowee smiled at the recollection. "You knows how Old Karl is . . . always looking out for a free drink."

"Then what?"

The small man slapped his hand on the counter top.

"He put a hunnert right there."

"That man?"

"Yes, Old Karl is still drinking from it."

"Yes," grinned DeKok, "Old Karl would never forget a face like that."

Little Lowee laughed heartily.

"Exactum! So when Old Karl tole me he had seen the geezer, I believed 'im rightaway."

"With a woman?"

"That's what Karl said . . . a lady."

"Did he talk to them?"

"I don't think so." Lowee shook his head. "He never said nuthin about it."

DeKok emptied his glass and slid of the stool.

"When you see Karl . . . send him over to the station."

Lowee looked doubtful.

"Iffen he want to. Old Karl don't like you guys that much."

DeKok winked.

"But he will come," he said with conviction. "Just tell him I'd like to keep things friendly."

* * *

Vledder placed a series of photographs in front of DeKok.

"Weelen went to work for us right-a-way, last night," he explained. "I think they're very good. You have to keep in mind it was only a simple camera. He did some nice enlargements. We got them in the morning papers"

DeKok nodded agreement.

"And the rest?"

"I took them back to the Sisters."

The old Inspector spread Bobby's photographs in front of him. Again he looked for a resemblance. There were some lines in the still unformed face he thought familiar. He had the vague, indefinite feeling that he had seen the face before ... somewhere, a long time ago. He scratched the back of his neck and then realized it could not have been all that long ago. Children changed rapidly.

A little old man entered the detective room. With short, decisive steps he unerringly aimed for DeKok's desk, carefully gathered his narrow pants above the knee and sat down with exaggerated care.

"Lowee said you wanted to see me," he announced.

DeKok glanced at the clock.

"Just quarter past nine ... you're early."

Old Karl snorted.

"I know you," he said moodily. "Any business with you I want to be rid of as soon as possible. At least I'll know where I'll stand." He patted himself on the chest. "It'll give me a restful feeling inside."

DeKok looked innocent.

"I have nothing on you. Anyway, they told me that you had retired."

The little old man stared at him, his eyes narrowed to suspicious slits.

"Is that what they said?"

"That's what they said," nodded DeKok, conviction in his voice. "Old Karl, they said, has retired ... full of regret and remorse."

The little old man cocked his head at the gray sleuth.

"Talk ... what does it get me? Why don't you just tell me what you need me for."

DeKok looked serious, the bantering undertone was gone.

"I wanted to talk to you about the couple you saw yesterday."

Old Karl shrugged his shoulders.

"I see so many couples," he evaded.

DeKok leaned closer.

"The man with the hundred."

"Oh . . . that one."

DeKok nodded.

"What time was that?"

"Two o'clock, maybe half past. I was on the bridge across Rear Fort Canal and they came out of a street, crossed the bridge toward Storm Alley."

"Did the man see you . . . recognize you?"

"I don't think so." Old Karl shook his head thoughtfully. "No, you see, I think they were quarreling."

"Quarrel . . . the man and that woman?"

Old Karl spread his hands in a resigned, sad gesture.

"It happens, you know. Also in those circles. I think he was pretty upset. He pulled rather harshly on the leash."

"Leash?"

"Yes," nodded Old Karl. "They had a dog with them. A big dog." He measured with his hand from the floor. "A Prince Bernard, but then all black."

"A *Saint* Bernard, you mean," smiled DeKok.

Old Karl nodded agreeably.

"As I said . . . with those big, padded feet."

"You couldn't be mistaken?" DeKok scratched the back of his neck as he looked intently at the old man.

Old Karl shook his wrinkled head.

"I am not yet senile," he exclaimed, offended. "I saw them as plain as day. They practically passed right by me as they crossed." He fell silent, moved restlessly in his chair. "Anything else you want?" he asked, "I still . . ."

DeKok gave him a friendly smile.

"No, thanks, off you go. I really appreciate you stopping by."

Old Karl hastily rose from his chair and left the room with a relieved look on his face.

DeKok watched him go. Then he pushed Bobby's photos together and placed them in a drawer.

"A dog," he murmured, hardly believing his own words.

Vledder came closer to the desk.

"You think they took Bobby, yesterday?"

DeKok looked at him.

"How could they know we had placed the child with the Sisters, for the time being?" He shook his head. "I don't think they had a clue. In any case," he added, as an afterthought, "they were walking in the wrong direction. I think they were on their way to Emperor Street."

Vledder grinned.

"What could they hope to find there? The house is empty."

DeKok ignored the remark and came hastily to his feet, an annoyed look on his face. Quickly he went over to the coat rack and grabbed his hat. Vledder looked after him with surprise.

"Where are you going?"

DeKok looked chagrined.

"Colette's funeral . . . it's at ten."

* * *

Vledder manoeuvered the old VW with his usual competence through the busy Amsterdam traffic. The old engine rattled and the exhaust protested with loud bangs.

DeKok was sprawled in the passenger seat, relaxed. Now that he had abandoned himself to a mechanical conveyance, there was nothing to do but relax. Either they arrived on time, or they did not. Either way, the outcome would rest with the fifty-seven horses behind the rear-seat. Right now, he thought, it sounded as if they were all fighting each other.

"Old Karl," he said suddenly, "is an old acquaintance of mine. He's real good with faces. He used to sell imitation rings ... looked like real gold, platinum ... nice, bright jewels. Dressed up with a heartrending tale, he used to sell them for good money to people with more greed than brains. Old Karl had to remember the faces, you see, he had to remember who he had cheated before . . . . a good memory for faces . . . it was a sort of life insurance policy."

"Has he really retired?"

"Maybe the odd ring," grinned DeKok, "if it happens to fall that way. There are always suckers looking for a good deal. They practically ask to be cheated."

The young Inspector glanced at his watch.

"We're going to be late," he said, concerned. "It's already quarter past ten." He glanced aside. "You want to go back to the barn? The ceremony will be finished by the time we reach Sorrow Fields."

"No," countered DeKok. "I'd like to take a look anyway. Sometimes the funerals don't go exactly like clockwork, either, you know. Maybe *they're* running late as well."

They drove through the gates of the cemetery and stopped near the office. Vledder rushed inside, but came back after a few seconds.

"They already left for the grave site," he panted.

The two Inspectors walked quickly in the indicated direction. They met a group of people coming back. DeKok recognized some of Colette's family members and pulled

Vledder into a branching path. He did not feel like a renewed confrontation with questions for which he had no answers.

They reached the grave site after a slight detour. They saw the broad back of a large man turned toward them as they came closer. DeKok restrained Vledder.

"Karel Karsemeyer," he whispered. "Leave him alone. Perhaps he's the only one who ever truly loved Colette."

The big man remained for a long while next to the grave site. Then he walked slowly away, his head bent in sorrow. DeKok looked around. There were a number of freshly dug graves all around with an abundance of flowers, ribbons and wreaths on freshly dug earth. It was completely still. Eery, suffocating, except for the occasional chirp of a bird. But that sound, too, seemed to be muffled as soon as it was uttered. Vledder looked at his older colleague.

"Had you expected anyone special?"

DeKok did not answer. His sharp ears had detected a strange sound, a bit further away, behind a thick clump of privets. It was the soft, almost ethereal rattling of tiny bells. Carefully he walked in the direction of the sound. Young Vledder close behind him.

Suddenly DeKok stopped. In front of them, among the gravestones, danced a girl. She wore a white blouse, open to the waist, and a multi-colored skirt that almost reached her ankles.

The long, black hair bobbed and curtsied with every movement of the slender body. She danced as if entranced. Her bare feet seemed to float above the grass.

12

The gray, mossy grave stones formed a remarkable setting for the dance. Monuments of death in a near magical circle. Caught in the ban of her movements, DeKok froze behind the privet hedge. The scene fascinated him. The strange thing was that her presence was not disturbing, not out of place. Her wild dance among the grave stones was not a dissonant, not a crass, coarse contradiction of life and death, but an accord.

After a few minutes DeKok turned around and walked back toward the graveled path. He suddenly thought about the evening, now three days ago, when he met her for the first time. "A grave," she had whispered, "that's what it's all about." And later she had added: ". . . yes, a grave for Colette. She can't stay that way." He pushed his little hat further back on his head and rubbed his face with a tired hand. Colette Maesen *had* her grave, but the puzzles surrounding her death had not been solved. Why did the girl have to die? It seemed so senseless, so, so unreasonable. Why did everybody say that Colette had a child when she had never even been pregnant? Who's child was it? How had she come by it? Why did the man with the graying temples have such interest in the boy? And above all . . . what had happened to the child?

Vledder caught up with him, his footsteps crunched on the gravel.

"The girl is crazy, I'm telling you," he said, pointing over his shoulder. "Believe me ... certifiable. We have to do something about that."

DeKok gave him a chilly look.

"What?" he asked, unperturbed.

The young Inspector shook his head in despair.

"Surely you can't allow that," he exclaimed, deeply offended. "That isn't allowed. We'll have to inform the cemetery personnel. You can't just let anybody dance among the grave stones."

"And why not?"

Vledder swallowed.

"You'll get into trouble with people who buried their loved ones here and ..."

DeKok waved away his objections.

"She'll be tired soon enough."

"Then what?"

"Then" smiled DeKok, "she'll take her little tambourine and go back to the Salvation Army. I discussed her with Major Bossart, yesterday. She said that Marianne's behavior is exemplary."

Vledder snorted.

"She belongs in an institution," he said roughly.

DeKok stopped suddenly in the center of the graveled path.

"Belongs," he said pensively. "Where *does* she belong?" He looked obliquely at his young friend. "What do we know about her? Just about nothing!"

"Marianne Vanburen," shrugged Vledder carelessly. "Just another homeless waif, from Breda, this time."

DeKok nodded slowly to himself.

"She was a little round when she was small. Her father called her Winnie the Pooh."

"That's important?" grimaced Vledder.

The obvious sarcasm seemed to escape DeKok. Slowly he walked on.

"Possibly," he murmured, "just possibly . . ."

When they reached the office, Vledder went inside and copied the exact information about the location of the grave, the type of stone and the number of the grave site. When he emerged from the building, DeKok looked at him.

"Did you mention it," he asked.

"Mention what?"

"That she's dancing?"

Vledder shook his head silently. He took the keys from a pocket and opened the door of the old VW. DeKok got in from the other side and they drove back to the city in silence.

The rain started to come down. DeKok looked at the big drops as they shattered on the windshield.

"We should have offered her a lift," he remarked.

"Who?"

"Marianne. It's quite a ways to walk, especially after you're tired from dancing."

Vledder engaged the wipers.

"You seem concerned."

DeKok ignored the remark. When Vledder got stuck in traffic, close to Warmoes Street, the gray sleuth got out of the car without a word and walked the rest of the way to the office.

Corporal Bikerk looked up as he entered the lobby.

"There's been a man waiting for you for more than half an hour. There were also a few women."

DeKok absorbed the information.

"Because of the newspaper article?"

"I guess so," nodded Bikerk. "I just sent them up. I think Dijk talked to them. The man insisted on waiting for you."

"Why?"

Bikerk shrugged his shoulders.

"I don't know. He wanted to see what you looked like, he said."

Grinning, DeKok rubbed the bridge of his nose with a little finger.

"Any news about the child?" he asked.

The Watch Commander shook his head.

"Nah, just a few vague phone calls from people who had seen a blond little boy somewhere. I passed them on to Dijk as well."

DeKok waved vaguely.

"All right, send the man up, will you?"

* * *

The man was short, wide and with a belly that protruded several inches in front of his belt buckle. The face was round and fleshy and the thin, strawberry blond hair was separated with a millimetric precise part. The startling green eyes sparkled merrily from behind rosy cheeks.

"You're Mr. DeKok?"

"With kay-oh-kay," responded DeKok almost automatically.

The man laughed heartily. His ample stomach jiggled in unison.

"She told me you would say that."

"Who?"

"My wife. She knows you. You helped her a few years back, some trouble with her first husband. She was separated at the time. My wife . . . she still often talks about you. A fine man she says always, Mr. DeKok." He smiled. "She told me to come see you. *Maybe I can do something in return,* she said."

"In return?"

He smiled again.

"Help you, you see, with your investigation."

DeKok looked at the man, considering.

"You want to help me?"

The man nodded agreement, the movement was positive and emphatic.

"I read it in the paper, this morning. About the child that disappeared. As soon as I opened the paper this morning and saw the photo, I told my wife: 'I know that little face.' I knew it at once, you see."

"From where?"

The man moved in his chair, leaned forward and placed both arms on the desk in a confidential, homely gesture. For the first time DeKok saw the thickness of the wrists, the hidden strength in the hands. The man narrowed his eyes in thought.

"It was about three months ago," he began. "I'm a truck driver, long-distance . . . Paris, Vienna, Prague. Usually I drive by myself. Sometimes I have another driver with me. Normally I *never* take hitch-hikers, certainly not across the border. It's nothing but trouble and you never know . . ."

"But you picked up hitch-hikers?" DeKok interrupted the stream of words.

"As I said," nodded the man. "About three months ago. I had just been to Hanover, in Germany, and was easing on back home. Just before the intersection near Bilthoven I saw two of them . . . girls. They waved their thumbs. I still don't know why I stopped. Perhaps because they were girls. Maybe because they had a small child with them, although they didn't look much older than children themselves."

DeKok's eyebrows rippled briefly.

"You gave them a ride?"

The man stared at him. It was not certain if he was surprised by the question, or if he wondered about what he thought he had seen on DeKok's forehead.

"Yes," he continued after a slight hesitation, "yes, I gave them a ride. How did you know?"

DeKok smiled wanly.

"I knew that *somebody* had given them a ride to Amsterdam, but that was all. I didn't know it was you." He scratched the bridge of his nose with a little finger. "What time did you pass Bilthoven?"

"Early. I guess about seven."

DeKok rummaged in an inside pocket and came out with a photo that he placed in front of the man.

"Was she one of them?"

The man looked and nodded.

"The other was slightly taller and had thick, black hair."

"And the child they had with them, was the same as the one in the paper?"

The man nodded again.

"Exactly. No doubt about it. I can still see that little face." He lifted Colette's photo from the desk and looked at it intently. "She looks different," he remarked.

"Taken after her death."

The round face looked confused.

"Dead?"

"Murdered," nodded DeKok nonchalantly.

The man swallowed. His hands moved restlessly and the corners of his mouth quivered.

"Murdered?" he repeated breathlessly.

"Three days ago."

"I have nothing to do with that."

The Inspector looked at the trucker with some surprise.

"But who says you do?"

The man took his mighty arms from the desk. He was pale, all color had drained from his face.

"And I don't want to have anything to do with it," he protested in a shaky voice. He shook his head. "Nossir, nothing! I came because of the child . . . not because of . . . m-murder."

DeKok gave him a winning smile.

"I understand. Please, don't distress yourself. I only want to know about the child." He gave the man an encouraging nod. "What is your name?"

"Vries, Peter Vries."

DeKok recovered Colette's photo and placed it in a drawer.

"You took the girls from Bilthoven to Amsterdam?"

"Yes."

"Where did you drop them off?"

"Admiral Quay . . . near the ferry, behind the Central Railroad Station."

"Did they say anything?"

"How do you mean?"

"Surely," gestured DeKok, "there must have been *some* conversation."

The man nodded absent-mindedly.

"We talked about traffic, dangers of the road, things like that. The one with the black hair said she'd seen an accident only the night before . . . three dead. She was still full of it." He chewed his lips thoughtfully. "And we talked about the child." Some color had come back in his cheeks. "I was a bit upset with those girls, children really. The child was hardly dressed at all . . . all naked from the waist down. And it was chilly that day, a bit blustery, you know. And they must have been standing there for some time. The poor thing had legs that were blue with cold. He shivered. I've got kids of my own and I really felt sorry for the kid. So I said: If you insist on hitch-hiking, find a home for the child first. I mean, really, anybody would have said the same thing. A child needs rest, warmth, protection. When I persisted, she became real nasty, told me that I belonged in a home, or something like that."

"Who said that?"

"The brunette." He waved vaguely. "The other one, the one from the picture, didn't say a whole lot. She just sat there, staring at the road. It was as if she were drunk."

"And she wasn't?"

"I didn't smell anything," laughed the man.

"Well," smiled DeKok, "not altogether the ideal travel companions, were they?"

The man shrugged his muscular shoulder.

"Ach," he said defensively, "they were, in a way. To be honest, I felt sorry for them. I slowed down on purpose. You see, it was nice and warm in the cab and I thought, as long as they're with me, they won't be cold." He smiled to himself, savoring the memory. "But with the brunette, the one with the black hair, well sir, it was a constant quarrel with her. About everything and nothing. At one point I said something like they should prohibit girls like them to have children." He rubbed the top of his head and laughed. "Stupid thing to say, of course, but you should have heard her. She said she didn't want to stay in the truck another moment, she wanted out, there and then... I had to stop at once." He moved uneasily in his chair. "Of course I didn't. I just let her rant and drove on."

He remained silent and looked at his nails. DeKok waited patiently. After a while the big man resumed.

"We, people, are so quick to judge," he continued, earning a warm spot in DeKok's heart. "After all, you never know how a girl like that gets into trouble. I was a bit sorry to have been so critical, you know. Anyway, when we got to Amsterdam, I took a tenner from my wallet and gave it them. Buy the little one a pair of pants, I said."

"Then what?"

"Well, sir, that was *also* the wrong thing to say. She became wild, screeched at me, cursed me up one side and down the other. I'm a truck driver and I'm used to all sorts of language, but I tell you, I was amazed at some of the things that came out of her mouth. *I don't need your filthy money*, she screamed. I've got plenty of clothes for the child." He looked at the gray sleuth with wide eyes. "Then she opened her rucksack," he went on, bemused, "and showed me all sorts of baby clothes . . . nice clothes, expensive little shirts, pants, sweaters, everything."

DeKok was surprised.

"But then . . . why was the child half-naked?"

The big trucker nodded in commiseration.

"Exactly, sir . . . why?"

13

"Were there a lot of people?"

Robert Antoine Dijk consulted his notes.

"An older man and four women. There were also a few phone calls."

"Anything usable among the lot?"

The young Inspector made a disappointed gesture.

"Apparently there are a lot of blond kids in our country that answer to the description."

DeKok scratched the bridge of his nose with a little finger. After a while he held the finger in the air and stared at it as if he saw it for the first time.

"Wasn't there *some* information?" he asked after a long pause.

"What do you mean?" Dijk was mystified.

DeKok lowered his finger and rose from behind his desk. He walked over to the wall with the large street map of Amsterdam.

"For instance . . . where had the child been seen?"

Dijk came over to stand next to him. He paused while he peered at the map.

"There were a couple of alerts from East." He said significantly. DeKok knew what he meant. The large living barracks in Amsterdam East had both alleviated the housing shortage and created its own problems. Not too long ago, he realized, a complete building had been practically wiped out when an Israeli freighter plane had crashed down on the densely populated area. Under certain conditions, the area was directly in the flight path of Schiphol, the Amsterdam airport.

"Oh?" prompted DeKok.

"A young couple, dressed casually, was seen with a blond child. The alerts came from the area of Sea Citizen Path." His finger moved over the map. "Then there was a call from North. A middle aged lady was seen in a shopping center. Then there was a report about a man with a crying child in a red Peugeot on Mercator Square. Also a call from a woman about an apparently abandoned child on a bench in Vondel Park and ..."

DeKok interrupted.

"That's a bit of a wide-spread area."

Dijk nodded agreement.

"In addition there are reports from Helmond, Zwolle, Alkmaar and Purmerend."

DeKok absorbed the names of the towns. Some were as far from Amsterdam as it was possible to be in Holland, without crossing the border. He looked inquiringly at Dijk.

"But," added the young man, "most of the reports, sightings I should say, were from the inner city."

"Where?"

Dijk pointed at the map as he enumerated.

"Here ... in the neighborhood of Gentlemen's Market, Harlem Street and Dry Ditch."

"What sort of sightings?" DeKok liked the word, it sounded positive.

Again Dijk consulted his notes.

"A gypsy with a child near Harlem Locks. A dirty man with a child in a laundromat. A strange young man with a blond child was seen by a shopkeeper in Inner Brewer Street. A man with . . ."

DeKok interrupted again. He raised his hand.

"What did he buy?"

"Who?"

"The strange young man with the child."

Robert Dijk looked abashed.

"I . . . I didn't ask. There were such a lot of calls," he added lamely.

"You have a name and an address?"

Dijk nodded.

"Beeskom, 104 Inner Brewer Street."

* * *

"Milk and rusks."

"That was all?"

Beeskom scratched his forehead while he looked at the ceiling for inspiration.

"A bar of chocolate and jam . . . a jar of strawberry jam."

"On the phone you mentioned 'a strange young man'. What was so strange about him?"

The shopkeeper smiled broadly.

"Well, I'm used to a few things. Especially lately. You get the oddest characters in your shop. In the old days it wasn't like that, you know. In those days you had your regular customers. You knew everybody and everybody knew you. But these days, these days . . . you get all kinds."

DeKok nodded resignedly. He had often noticed it himself.

"But this young man was particularly strange?"

Beeskom gestured apologetically.

"Well, you shouldn't judge, you know," he said while DeKok reflected that this was the second time someone had voiced his own sentiments back to him. He waited patiently for the shopkeeper to continue. "When I say *strange*," the man went on, "I mean the way he handled the child. Strange, you know, as if he wasn't used to dealing with children. You could just see it. I've five of my own and . . ."

"You said he was not used to dealing with children?" DeKok tried to stick to the facts.

"Exactly. Or shops. He wanted to pick up the shopping before I could even put it in a bag. In the process he almost dropped the child. It was odd."

"How often has he been in your shop?"

"Just once."

"Any idea where he's from?"

Beeskom spread his arms wide.

"That's hard to say."

"A squatter? An abandoned building?"

The shopkeeper shook his head.

"There are hardly any abandoned buildings around here. Good thing too. Most of the empty ones that *are* here have been shut off with masonry until they knock it down. I would try closer to Harlem Street, if that's what you're after. They have a couple of buildings there that have not yet been declared uninhabitable and they rent rooms. I *did* see him go in that direction with the child."

DeKok nodded his thanks.

"If that young man ever comes back . . ."

"I have your phone number," grinned Beeskom.

* * *

They walked from Inner Brewer Street to Harlem Street. Vledder glanced at his mentor.

"You know what houses the shopkeeper was talking about?"

"Yes," nodded DeKok, "unfortunately I do. Unbelievable conditions. You can hardly call them 'rented rooms'. Just dirty cubicles, often with plywood walls. They're cheap, it's their only virtue. They're mostly occupied by guest-workers."

"And you think Bobby is there?"

"Possibly." DeKok shrugged his shoulders. "We have to try *something*. Most of the reports are concentrated in this area. Milk, rusks, jam . . . it could mean food for a child. If that child happens to be Bobby . . ." He did not complete the sentence, but stopped in front of a decrepit, old door and pushed it open. A large pile of mail was thrown in a heap on the granite floor. The building did not have individual mail boxes. The gray sleuth picked up the mail and looked at the names of the addressees. Vledder peered over his shoulder.

"Anybody you know?"

"No, I don't recognize anybody." He placed the letters and mail back on the floor where he had found them and walked toward the narrow staircase, Vledder close behind.

On the next floor an arrow had been roughly painted on the dirty wall. "Report Here", it commanded. They walked in the direction of the arrow and reached a closed door at the end of the hall. DeKok knocked on the door and entered almost simultaneously. An older woman was seated at a table almost covered with playing cards. A recently lit cigarette drooped from between thin lips. She gave the intruders an annoyed look.

"Hello . . . Aunt Marie," waved DeKok.

She placed a card on the table. Its progress had momentarily stopped when the two cops entered.

"What you want?" she growled.

DeKok looked at her sadly.

"Would it hurt you to be a little friendlier?" he asked.

"I ain't never happy to see you."

"But," smiled DeKok, "I've always been nice to you. Surely I would have thought you remembered me with fondness."

With some difficulty she rose from her chair and snorted contemptuously.

"What you want?" she repeated, her hands on her hips. "You looking for somebody?"

The old Inspector made a vague gesture.

"A young man . . . with a child."

"You too?"

DeKok managed to hide his surprise. He gave her a searching look.

"What do you mean . . . you too?"

She squinted at him.

"There was a woman here this morning."

"What time?"

"About half past nine."

"What sort of woman?"

She shrugged her shoulders, an uncooperative look on her face.

"A nice person . . . a lady . . . in a manner of speaking."

"She came here and, just like me, asked for a young man and a child?"

"Yes."

"Then what?"

"I sent her upstairs. The attic . . . room nine."

"What else?"

She looked at him, the suspicious look had been replaced by genuine confusion.

"Nothing else . . . nothing. I haven't seen her since."

* * *

They climbed the stairs. Aunt Marie in front, a large bundle of keys in one hand. Droopy stockings hung around her ankles and her wide feet were covered by large men's slippers. Her free hand was cramped around the banister. With difficulty she dragged herself up the stairs.

On the next floor she stopped, catching her breath.

"Of course she could have slipped by me," she said after a pause filled with deep breathing. "They all do it sometimes. Especially when they owe rent."

DeKok nodded his understanding, but indicated for her to proceed. With a long-suffering look in her eyes she complied, but she stopped again halfway up the stairs.

"Usually I don't allow children," she explained. "But that guy said that his wife was carrying on with another man and didn't make any attempt to hide it from the child . . . finally he couldn't stand it any longer and he had taken the child and left."

"How much higher?" asked DeKok, trying to see in the gloom.

"Two more flights," she answered and took another labored step closer to their goal. "But let me tell you, if the child is going to be a bother, he *and* his child can just leave. I'm not running a kindergarten."

"Didn't you read the paper this morning?"

"Nah, I'd rather play cards," she answered, shaking her head. "I don't need the paper. It's full of bad news. I have enough bad news in my own life." She glanced back over her shoulder. "Something the matter with the child?"

DeKok did not answer.

When they finally reached the attic floor, she shuffled down a narrow corridor toward a door with the numeral nine painted on the bare wood. She took a few more minutes to get her breathing under control and then knocked on the door.

There was no response.

She knocked again and listened with her ear against the door.

"Probably not in," she said, turning toward the cops. She balled a bony hand into a fist and banged on the door. After the sound had ebbed away, only silence remained.

After a few more seconds, she grabbed the greasy doorknob and opened the door. DeKok watched her back and deduced from the sudden spasm that something had frightened her. He placed a hand on her shoulder and gently forced her back into the hall. Her wrinkled face was gray and her eyes seemed to protrude from the sockets.

"Oh, God," she whispered shakily, "Oh, dear God."

DeKok pushed her aside and with his foot pressed the door wider. The body was about two feet from the disordered bed. It was Fred Mellenkamp. The dead eyes were wide open and stared at the ceiling. A strange, twisted grin was on his lips. It was as if he were trying to understand a joke, a joke for which the punch line was missing.

Vledder peeked over DeKok's shoulder.

"Dead?"

DeKok nodded slowly.

"Murdered."

14

Inspector DeKok allowed his sharp gaze to roam through the attic room. Almost without being aware of it, he noticed everything. He had a photographic memory for scenes like that. Afterward he could accurately name and place every item in the room.

The light from the angled attic window illuminated a low table with a yellowed, imitation marble top. Two bowls, a dirty plate and a bottle of milk, one quarter empty, were placed on the table. Bread crumbs and an open packet of margarine surrounded the open jam jar. A white plastic spoon was stuck in the jam and a few rusks were missing from the roughly torn roll.

A small piece of gas pipe, about three feet long, was lying next to the head of the victim. At the end, near the elbow joint, it was sticky with blood and some blond hair. DeKok knelt down next to the corpse and looked at the wounds. They glimmered rosily from beneath the light hair. Gently he closed the dead man's eyes. Then he stood up and searched for blood spatters. He found them low, near to the ground, below the knee of the roof-line. He pointed them out to Vledder.

"What do you think?" he asked.

Vledder studied the situation.

"The second . . . and successive blows were administered," he said in the curious jargon of official reports, "while the victim was already on the floor."

DeKok nodded agreement.

"I think he was surprised while asleep."

Vledder, never loath to state the obvious, looked at his mentor.

"You mean he was in bed when he received the first blow?"

DeKok pushed his lower lip forward.

"The first blow never results in blood spatters. That's why there's no sign of blood on the bed. When the victim, possibly as a result of the initial blow, rolled onto the floor, the killer hit again . . . in the same spot."

Vledder sighed elaborately

"And hence the blood spatters," he added.

DeKok rubbed his chin in a pensive gesture.

"Remains to be seen, of course, if the victim was indeed asleep when he was hit for the first time. It's possible that he was under the assumption he had nothing to fear from his visitor, whether male or female. He could have just stayed in bed while he conversed at leisure."

Vledder looked at the victim and shook his head in pity.

"Whatever . . . Fred Mellenkamp didn't have a chance." He pressed his lips together. Then he added: "It's about time we identify the killer. Who knows who's going to be the next victim . . ."

DeKok's eyebrows rippled briefly, but Vledder was too absorbed in his own thoughts to notice. A rarity and he would have regretted his inattention if he had known.

"Are you suggesting that the same person who killed Colette Maesen is responsible for this?" DeKok asked, gesturing around the room.

"It's the same type of murder," asserted Vledder with conviction.

DeKok did not react. He turned to the landlady who had stayed just outside the open door of the room. Aunt Marie seemed to have recovered from the initial shock and was again her usual garrulous self. She looked less pale.

"What time did he come in, yesterday?" asked DeKok, pointing at the corpse.

"Three, half past." She sounded unconcerned. "Maybe later," she added carelessly.

DeKok reached for the photo in an inner pocket. He showed her Bobby's picture, so fortuitously provided by the good sisters.

"Did he have this child with him?"

She took the picture from his hand and studied it

"Yes, this child . . . and a bag of groceries."

"Did he have any visitors?"

"When?"

"Yesterday."

She shook her head.

"He left for a while, about eight. He had to make a phone call and he asked me to look after the child."

"And you did?"

She nodded.

"I looked in on him." The hard lines in her face softened somewhat. "He was sleeping so peacefully. Just like a little cherub."

"With the door open? I mean, the door wasn't locked?"

She shook her head.

"That wasn't possible."

DeKok looked at the lock. It looked in good working order.

"Why not?" he asked, surprise in his voice.

She grinned crookedly.

"The previous occupant took the keys with him."

"But then you could have given him a spare key."

She grinned again, knowingly, and shook the large bunch of keys in her hands.

"I prefer to remain boss in my own house," she explained. "If I had given him my spare key, I wouldn't have had a key myself. There's only two keys for every door."

DeKok nodded to himself. In this sort of rooming house it was simply unthinkable to have extra keys made.

"What time did he come back, after he had left?"

"About ten."

"Alone?"

She shrugged her shoulders.

"He just put his head around the door to say he was back. I don't know if there was anybody with him." She grinned wickedly. "I don't care, I don't run a boarding school. As long as they pay the rent, they do what they want."

"And did he pay the rent?"

She sighed bitterly.

"Tomorrow," she said, shaking her head. "He was going to pay me tomorrow. He said he was coming into a lot of money."

DeKok was astonished.

"And you believed him?"

She nodded slowly, staring at the corpse.

"He said it in a way that made it sound true."

* * *

DeKok had tired feet. He leaned back in his chair and with a groan he lifted his legs on top of the desk. A sharp pain started in his toes and worked its way up to his calves, where knives seemed to rip the flesh apart. It made him melancholy. He knew what the pain signified. When a case was not making progress, when things did not go smoothly, when he was on the wrong path, or saw no solution . . . the pains began. He had learned to live with it.

"Bobby is gone," he said somberly. "The killer took him away." He sighed, a concerned look on his face. "The thought that the child is in the hands of someone who has killed so mercilessly makes me fear the worst."

Vledder looked up from his computer terminal. As usual he had added the latest information to his growing files of facts. He also, DeKok knew, kept a running commentary in at least three different files in the computer. One of the benefits of his association with the young Inspector, contemplated DeKok, was that he never had to bother about reports anymore. Vledder seemed to be able to whip up any kind of report for any purpose at the flick of a wrist. The young man had tried to explain what he was doing. But all the talk about files, sub-files, headings, standard language, input, output and even something called "throughput" had only caused DeKok to have an overwhelming desire for a cognac. Vledder had never tried to explain again.

"So, we assume that Fred Mellenkamp took the child in Wester Park?" the young man queried.

"Yes," nodded DeKok. "He must have followed Sister Angelica and when he saw his chance, he took the child and just walked away. After all, he was no stranger to Bobby, so Bobby was likely to trust him."

"But why did he want the child?"

"Obvious," gestured DeKok, rubbing his painful calves, "he wanted to sell him. We can safely take it that he called somebody that same evening. Someone who was willing to pay the price." He paused. "Perhaps he did it on contract."

Vledder's eyes widened.

"That woman," he exclaimed enthusiastically. "Of course, she ordered a child and Fred was going to deliver. The woman who visited Aunt Marie."

"Possibly," said DeKok, not committing himself.

The young Inspector stood up from behind his desk. His youthful face was tense.

"She had to be the one," he said earnestly. "Of course. She killed Mellenkamp. They had words about the kidnapping, an argument. When they couldn't agree, she hit him with the pipe and took the child."

DeKok pulled at his lower lip and let it plop back. It was an annoying sound and he repeated it several times.

"But," he said after a while, "aren't you the one who surmised that Colette and Fred had both been killed by the same killer?"

"Yes."

"Then . . . why did the woman kill Colette?"

Vledder was not discouraged.

"For the same reason. Colette started the negotiations for the child. Except Bobby wasn't there, or the woman couldn't find him in that hall closet."

DeKok stared at him with unblinking eyes.

"So she took the koala bear as a sort of consolation prize?" he asked sarcastically. "So that someone could conclude she was on the right track?"

Vledder hesitated.

"Is that so strange?" he asked after a long pause.

DeKok slowly shook his head.

"It's a nice theory," he said pensively. "Certainly we should consider it. But it raises another question . . . who is the mysterious figure in the background."

Vledder gestured expansively, not seeing a problem.

"Somebody who is willing to pay enough for the child that it's worth killing for."

The phone rang. Vledder, who was closer, lifted the receiver. After a moment he handed it to DeKok.

"DeKok," said the older man resignedly.

Suddenly he lifted his feet from the desk and sat bold upright.

"What?" he exclaimed, totally surprised. "Gone? When? Left no word? What time? Thanks." He replaced the receiver. His face was serious.

Vledder looked expectantly.

"What's the matter?"

"That was Major Bossart. Marianne Vanburen left last night. She took all her belongings and has not returned."

Vledder shook his head and laughed mirthlessly.

"Only this morning she was still dancing on Colette's grave."

DeKok ignored the remark. He stared into the distance. He was trying to recall a scene, a particular thought association. There was a dreamy look in his eyes.

"She was dancing," he said softly. "She danced."

Robert Antoine Dijk entered the detective room in a hurry. He took a chair next to DeKok's desk and pulled out his notebook.

"Fred . . . or Frederik Hendrik Mellenkamp," he read aloud, "was born twenty seven years ago in Amersfoort. His family moved to Amsterdam when he was fourteen where he completed High School. His father urged him to study Law and he was involved in a number of student organizations. This led to a difference of opinion with his authoritarian father and he left home. Although his mother later managed to arrange a reconciliation, Fred never moved back into the parental home. He visited at irregular times, usually when his finances had been depleted."

"Work?"

"For a while he was connected with a so-called Law Store, you know, a store-front operation, managed by lawyers and paralegals that give free, or cheap, legal advice."

"Here in Amsterdam?"

"Indeed. Then he worked for a while at a temp service. They also had nothing detrimental to say about him."

"Drugs?"

Dijk shook his head.

"I inquired among the better known junkies and in some of the drug stores. It wasn't a complete search, but so far nobody knew him. He isn't known as either a dealer, or a user."

"You visited his parents?"

"Yes," nodded Robert Antoine. "You wanted some additional information about him, didn't you. What with all the furor about the missing child, I left it for last."

DeKok looked at the young, eager Inspector.

"I'm sure that among your more exotic wardrobe you have a dark suit and a subdued tie."

Dijk looked suspicious, but agreed that it was so.

"Then go put it on," said DeKok tiredly, "and go back to the parents. Tell them their son has passed away."

Robert swallowed, his adam's apple bobbed up and down and he looked pale.

"Mellenkamp is . . . eh, dead?"

"I'm afraid so," said DeKok. "Vledder and I found him this morning in an attic room at Harlem Street. He was murdered."

"But," protested Dijk, obviously confused, "he only called his father last night."

"What time?"

"Near ten."

"From where?"

Dijk shrugged his shoulders.

"According to his father, from some bar. There was loud music in the background."

"I see . . . why did he call?"

"Fred said that he was leaving Amsterdam for a while." Dijk gestured vaguely. "He just called to tell his parents not to worry about him if he didn't show up for a while."

"Did he say where he was going?"

"No."

DeKok rubbed a hand over his face. Then he turned around and started to pace up and down the large room, subconsciously avoiding obstacles and other occupants. He avoided his surroundings with practiced ease, but was not really aware of it. The pain in his feet had disappeared and his brain worked at top speed. The second murder had momentarily surprised him and had given an unexpected twist to the case.

After a while he stopped in front of Vledder's desk and held a finger up in the air.

"Fred Mellenkamp," he said in an infuriatingly didactic tone of voice, "called his father around ten o'clock in the evening and said that he was leaving Amsterdam for a while. According to Aunt Marie it was near ten when he stuck his head around the door to say he was back. That leaves very little time. Therefore, the place from where he called must have been close to the boarding house." He turned toward Robert Antoine. "Inform Mellenkamp's parents. For details you refer them to me. Please be careful and tactful." He paused. "Then you go to Harlem Street and find out from what bar Fred called his father. Perhaps he made other calls . . . calls for which he had to pay."

"And then?" asked Dijk, getting to his feet.

"Then you come straight back here."

As soon as Dijk had left, DeKok turned back to Vledder.

"Do you have Mellenkamp's belongings?"

"What belongings?" In addition to being obvious, Vledder could also be obtuse.

"The belongings from the attic room," explained DeKok patiently.

Vledder pointed toward the floor below.

"In the evidence room."

"Did you go through them?"

Vledder made a helpless gesture.

"There was nothing of any value. I mean, nothing that could help us."

"No wallet, no notes, no notebook, pocket calendar, receipt?"

Vledder shook his head, an apologetic look on his face.

"I went over everything most carefully. Not a thing." He opened a drawer in his desk. "Here is the list." As he spoke the words, one hand flew over his keyboard and as he handed the handwritten list to DeKok, the duplicate appeared on the screen. As DeKok looked at the list in his hand, Vledder elaborated, reading off the screen.

"A bottle with milk, two bowls, a dirty plate and a jam jar with jam. All have been dusted for prints. Some of the prints were identified as those of Mellenkamp and some of the smaller, childsize prints were undoubtedly from Bobby. In addition there was a pair of jeans, an Army jacket, a T-shirt, a pair of shoes with crooked heels and a pair of knit socks . . . goat wool, according to the experts. He wore no underwear.."

"And there were no papers in the pockets of the jacket?"

Vledder looked annoyed.

"What are you after?" he asked in a long-suffering tone of voice. "Look for yourself."

DeKok shook his head. He grabbed a chair and seated himself.

"Look," he explained patiently, "Fred Mellenkamp called his father last night. We can reasonably assume that he knew the number by heart. But he also must have made contact with the woman who showed up the next morning."

Vledder nodded his understanding.

"You mean, *that* number could have been written down somewhere?"

"Exactly. It could be a lead. Of course it's possible he knew her name and just looked up the number in the phone book. But in that case the woman was more than likely from Amsterdam."

"Why?"

"Usually there are no phone books for other cities in a bar."

"Of course," grinned Vledder. "Certainly not in the type of bars you find in the area of Harlem Street. But . . . he could have called information."

DeKok scratched the back of his neck. There was a look on his face that suggested extreme weariness.

"You're right," he said, depressed. "It's a difficult case. It's hardly likely that an operator would remember the call and with all this direct dialing these days, the actual call was certainly not logged in a way that's easily accessible to us. But maybe Robert Antoine will get lucky. He should be able to find that bar. And then we can lift their phone records."

Suddenly Vledder stood up. His eyes were wide.

"But there *was* a number," he panted. "On his arm."

DeKok looked up in surprise.

"On his arm?"

Vledder nodded with emphasis.

"On his inner arm. I saw it when they undressed him at the morgue. I thought it was a concentration camp number. It was in the same place and in blue." He looked sheepish. "You know how your mind wanders." He paused. "But of course, he's much too young to have been in a concentration camp," he concluded lamely.

"Do you have the number?"

Vledder bit his lip.

"No . . . I thought to get it tomorrow, during the autopsy."

DeKok stood up and went to the coat rack. He took his old hat off the hook and planted it firmly on his head.

"Where are you going?" asked Vledder, suspecting the answer.

"To the morgue."

15

DeKok pulled back the sheet. Again he was struck by the strange, surprised grin on the face of the dead man. With some difficulty he tore his gaze away.

Young Vledder lifted the left arm of the corpse. The numbers were clearly visible, on the inside of the arm, just above the wrist.

"One-two-five-nine-one," he read out loud.

DeKok wrote the number in his notebook and put the book back in his pocket. Vledder could not help but notice that only a few pages of DeKok's notebook had been used and he knew for a fact that DeKok had used the same book for several years. It was a tribute to Vledder's secretarial skills and DeKok's phenomenal memory.

Meanwhile DeKok had walked over to the wash basin in the corner and held a towel under the tap. With the damp tip of the towel he softly rubbed over the numbers. The numbers slowly disappeared. The gray sleuth looked at the bluish color that remained on the towel.

"Ball point," he stated.

Vledder nodded.

"A five-digit number," he remarked.

DeKok threw the towel in a basket.

"If it's a phone number, we can forget about the big cities. They usually have six or more digits." Vledder smiled faintly. DeKok was known for his abhorrence of all things modern, but always seemed to know the crucial bits of information.

"Now we need to know the area code," continued DeKok. He tugged the sheet back in place, covering the corpse. The gesture was slow, respectful, with a certain piety as he took a last look at the strange grin.

"What time is the autopsy?"

"Four in the afternoon. That's the earliest Dr. Rusteloos is available."

DeKok pursed his lips.

"Then we can take care of the official identification in the morning. Robert Antoine can handle that. He already knows the parents."

Vledder switched off the light as they left the morgue. They crossed the wide pavement toward the car. DeKok pulled his hat deeper into his eyes. It was raining. A soft, ground-soaking, all-pervasive drizzle. They got into the car and drove away in the direction of Nassau Quay. DeKok looked at the sweeping window wipers.

"One-two-five-nine-one," he murmured in rhythm with the wipers. "Fred no doubt knew what city to call."

"Obviously," agreed Vledder.

"And if he knew the city," concluded DeKok, "he could look up the area code in any phone book." He paused. "One of the advantages of living in a small country," he added.

"But it doesn't help us," snorted Vledder. "Without the area code the number is useless. Fine," he went on bitterly, "we can call every area code with five-digit numbers and try it. But that still leaves about a few hundred possibilities. In the short run it's less than useless."

DeKok pushed his ridiculous little hat further back on his head.

"Colette Maesen is dead," he said soberly. "And Fred Mellenkamp is dead. Both of them knew who was interested in the child." He pushed himself up in his seat, looked around and recognized the Roses Canal. "Go on to Old Front Fort Canal," he added evenly.

Vledder looked at him.

"Whatever for?"

DeKok sank back in his seat.

"For a talk," he said languidly, "with the major."

* * *

"Good evening, gentlemen." The slightly hoarse voice of the major sounded warm. "Are you here to restore our Marianne to us?"

DeKok shook his head sadly.

"I don't know where she is. But I do have the vague feeling that she's in trouble."

"Why?"

DeKok gestured.

"This morning we found a young man, a young man who seemed to be involved with Marianne for some time. He was murdered."

"And she has something to do with that?"

The gray sleuth spread wide his arms in a display of helplessness.

"That's what I'm wondering about." He paused and looked earnestly at the woman. "There is," he began, hesitating, searching for the words, "a certain knowledge, call it a secret, surrounding the child. As far as we know at least three people were definitely aware of the secret . . . Colette Maesen, a young woman, addicted to heroin . . . Fred Mellenkamp, the young man I just told you about . . . and Marianne."

He remained silent, stared into the distance.

"Colette Maesen and Fred Mellenkamp," he went on, "both met a violent death within a short period of each other."

Major Bossart sighed.

"I understand. You're afraid that Marianne is also in danger."

DeKok nodded slowly.

"It's important that we find her as soon as possible. I don't think she's aware of the situation. She probably has no inkling from what direction the danger is coming."

"Do *you* know?"

DeKok lowered his head.

"Regretfully I have to admit that we're completely in the dark." He paused again, looked up. "Did you have a chance to talk with Marianne?"

Major Bossart shook her head.

"I didn't have much contact with her, personally. Corporal Anna did. She was very much concerned about Marianne's fate."

DeKok rubbed the bridge of his nose with a little finger. It was almost a shy gesture under the circumstances.

"Is there any chance we could speak to Corporal Anna?"

Major Bossart hesitated, she looked doubtful.

"You must understand that the Salvation Army was never intended to be an adjunct to the police. If Marianne spoke in confidence . . ."

DeKok raised a protesting hand.

"We have no intention of embarrassing anyone. Certainly we respect the limits of . . . eh, of conscience. But we're after small things, hints really. A loose remark, an observation, small hints that may help us."

Major Bossart came to a decision.

"Please remain seated. I'll fetch Corporal Anna."

She left and returned shortly thereafter, accompanied by a young woman dressed in the uniform of the Salvation Army. Vledder could not find anything on the uniform that indicated a rank. DeKok estimated her to be in her early twenties. She had a friendly, open face and a happy look in her light gray eyes.

Major Bossart made the introductions.

"These gentlemen are from the police and they want to ask you some questions about Marianne Vanburen."

The old Inspector, who had risen when the two women entered the small office, now made a formal bow.

"My name is DeKok," he said, "with kay-oh-kay." He pointed a thumb at Vledder, who was standing next to him. "My colleague, Dick Vledder."

The young woman looked at the two men with a penetrating glance. Her gaze shifted from DeKok to Vledder and back again.

"How can I help you?' she asked.

DeKok smiled.

"Why don't we sit down?" He took a chair and held it for her with the charm of a diplomat from an earlier age and the expertise of a head-waiter in an expensive restaurant. When she was seated and the major had resumed her place behind the desk, DeKok turned to the young Corporal.

"The major told us that you were rather concerned about Marianne and that you had a good rapport with her."

"Marianne," said the young woman seriously, "is a fascinating girl."

"You talked with her a lot?"

"She talked with me, to be more accurate." She smiled.

"Isn't that the same thing?" asked DeKok ingenuously.

She shook her head with a decisive movement.

"Marianne," she explained, "has a rather closed character. She works everything out by herself, without bringing it out in the open. If I tried to make her talk, the conversation would always be shifted, somehow. Instead of me asking her, *she* would ask me. Instead of telling me about her life, she forced me to reveal confidences."

"Such as?"

Corporal Anna moved in her chair, brought her knees closer together and gave another tug at her skirt.

"What I thought about the world in general . . . about God, about my parents, about men, about sex . . ."

DeKok nodded to himself.

"Did she never say anything about herself? About her experiences?"

The hands moved in her lap.

"She was with us only a short time." It sounded like an apology. "Two, maybe three days. Marianne wasn't ready yet. Trust between people must have time to grow, to mature."

DeKok bowed his head in compliment.

"You're absolutely right," he said sincerely. "It takes time." He made an inviting gesture in her direction. "What was *your* opinion of her?"

She looked pained.

"That's a difficult question. Marianne had lived a full life, an eventful life. That's for sure. A lot of disappointments. She was often depressed . . . as if something bothered her, hung over her. One day . . . we were having coffee . . . she suddenly asked if I had ever seen a child burn."

"Seen a child burn?" asked DeKok, keeping his voice even although his heart seemed to skip a beat.

"That's what she asked: *Have you ever seen a child burn?*" There was no question of doubting the sincerity of the young Salvation Army soldier.

"What did you say?"

"I said no, of course, thank God for that. But then she said: *It's something you never forget. Just for that they should make cars illegal.*"

* * *

Vledder approached the desk with two steaming mugs of coffee. He placed one in front of his old friend.

"For you," he said warmly, "lots of sugar."

DeKok looked grateful. He lifted the hot mug with both hands and slurped comfortably. His lined face relaxed.

"Marianne," he said softly, "what do we really know about her?"

Vledder sat down on the other side of the old man's desk.

"You asked the same thing on the way back from Colette's funeral," he smiled. "That same morning I called Breda. The police there knew nothing about her. She also did not appear in the Town Registry. There are several Vanburens, but none have a daughter that age."

DeKok looked surprised.

"You didn't tell me that," he said. There was censure in his voice.

Vledder put his coffee down and spread his arms.

"I didn't take it seriously," he apologized. "I thought I'd ask her myself for clarification. After all, I had no way of knowing she would disappear just like that."

"But she did say she came from Breda, didn't she?"

"Yes, that's what she said all right. But perhaps that was a lie. Maybe even the name Vanburen is fictitious." He pressed his lips together and managed to snort at the same time. "I told you," he said after a brief pause, "I thought she was a strange girl right from the beginning. Whoever dances in a cemetery?"

DeKok pursed his lips, took another slurp of coffee.

"Not enough reason to call her strange," he observed.

Vledder stuck out his chin.

"Well, it is for me," he said, a challenge in his voice. "Also, it's actually all her fault."

"What!?"

Vledder gesticulated.

"Everything . . . the death of Colette, Fred's murder. It's all a result of her plan. She was the one to prevail on Colette to ask the rich acquaintance for money."

"On the basis of a lie," grinned DeKok. "That rich acquaintance was supposed to be Bobby's father. But Colette lied as well. We know she never was pregnant."

Vledder persisted.

"But that guy had no way of knowing," he protested. "That guy could easily be led to believe that a child resulted from his relationship with Colette."

DeKok looked at his young friend, partner and colleague.

"Bobby?" he asked slowly, a sweet smile on his face. "The child of which he had a picture?"

"Yes."

DeKok shook his head.

"Colette Maesen *never* had a relationship. I mean *not* with a rich, distinguished gentleman, graying at the temples. The one who came to Lowee's bar."

Vledder's eyes narrowed, he prepared himself to argue.

"Oh, no?" he asked.

DeKok sighed elaborately.

"I've hinted at it before . . . you weren't listening carefully when we interviewed Karel Karsemeyer." He gestured toward Vledder. "When did Colette leave Karel?"

"Two years ago."

"How long was she with him?"

"Over a year."

"Excellent," praised DeKok, "really excellent. He picked her up from the gutter and kept her in his house for over a year. A year in which, in order to help her kick the habit, he watched her practically day and night." He leaned forward.

"And how old is Bobby?"

"One and a half, two years."

DeKok smiled thinly.

"So, you see, if Bobby was supposed to be Colette's child ... only Karel Karsemeyer could have been the father. There was no room for another relationship."

Vledder looked flabbergasted.

"Then how," he stammered, "did she latch on the 'rich' acquaintance ... and why did he react the way he did?"

DeKok looked at him with admiration in his eyes.

"Those," he said slowly, "are two very intelligent questions."

* * *

"You're late, aren't you?"

Robert Antoine Dijk plopped down in the chair next to the desk. He was pale and his nostrils quivered.

"I'll never do that again," he said passionately and shook his head for emphasis. "Never again."

DeKok looked at him searchingly.

"It was that bad?"

"I really did my best." The young Inspector swallowed. "I tried to be as careful and as tactful as possible. I had a serious face and told them that something had happened ... that something serious had happened to their son. But it was as if they didn't understand me, didn't *want* to understand me ... as if I were talking about a stranger." He swallowed again. "They just stared at me, both of them ... forced me to tell them all the details." Dijk took his head in his hands. "It was sheer torture. When I finally told them the truth, that their son had been murdered, they went berserk. Especially the mother ranted and raved. She screamed out loud, banged her head on the table. Finally, I fled to the neighbors for help."

"And they helped?"

"Dear people," sighed Robert Antoine, nodding his head. "They knew the family well. I spoke briefly with the man. He didn't seem very surprised. According to him, Fred Mellenkamp was no good at all. He had always caused a lot of suffering for his parents. There had been a number of things: affairs with women, thefts and fraud with employers."

"Anything reported to the police?"

Dijk shook his head.

"The police were left out of it, according to the neighbor. Everything was covered by the cloak of love, his words. The shortages were reimbursed and it was never discussed again."

"A good cover," said DeKok pensively.

"What?"

"The cloak of love. I like that."

Robert Antoine stared at the older man. DeKok smiled at him.

"This was a rough one, I agree," he said soothingly. "But you'll do it again. It's part of the job. The least agreeable part, no doubt. The victims are out of it, but the survivors are always left to cope. You did the right thing. If you can't find relatives, call the neighbors. People who have just been confronted with grief, need familiar faces around them, need to cry together. And a good neighbor is better than a distant friend, as the saying goes."

Dijk smiled wanly. Some color came back into his cheeks. DeKok's platitudes could not hide the implied praise for his behavior.

"The neighbors promised to keep an eye on things," he said.

DeKok nodded his understanding.

"Those affairs with women . . . were there consequences?"

"How do you mean?"

"Children."

"I'm sorry, I didn't ask. I just didn't pursue the subject. It was a panic situation. After the news had penetrated, the parents were unapproachable. Not a sensible word to be had."

"And the neighbor?"

Dijk made an apologetic gesture.

"I was under the impression that he was a bit sorry he had said as much. It was more an immediate reaction. After that he evaded me, concentrated on his neighbors."

DeKok scratched the bridge of his nose with a little finger.

"The first time you saw the parents . . . did you discuss women at that time?"

"No, hardly at all. I just asked if Fred was married, or had been married. They said no and that was the end of the subject."

DeKok grimaced.

"Surely you're aware that a man can have a child without being married?"

"You mean, that a child could have been the result of one of the affairs?"

"Of course." said DeKok.

"Fred Mellenkamp wasn't a father." Dijk shook his head resolutely. "In any case he didn't have a child his parents knew about. Otherwise they would most certainly have told me. I also didn't see a photo anywhere."

"Well, a lot of people keep family pictures only in the bedroom," observed DeKok.

Before Dijk could comment, Vledder interrupted.

"Are you saying," he said with suspicion in his voice, "that Bobby is the child of Fred Mellenkamp?"

The gray sleuth spread wide his arms in a gesture of surrender.

"Bobby is definitely *not* Colette's child. That's the only thing we know for sure. Apart from that, *anything* is possible."

"DeKok is right," nodded Dijk. "The child could even be Marianne's."

Vledder stood up, agitated, a dissatisfied look on his face.

"The child doesn't belong to either Marianne or Fred," he exclaimed, irritated. "The child has been stolen . . . for ransom. It's a plain case of kidnapping."

"By three people?"

"Yes, Colette, Marianne and Fred. How they divided the various responsibilities I don't know. But all three were involved."

Robert Antoine thought for a moment.

"But," he objected, "why have the parents not notified the police? There's nothing known about the theft, the kidnapping of a child. You know yourself, if that was the case, the police wires would be humming."

Vledder sighed impatiently.

"Because they were afraid something would happen to the child." He waved his arms to add strength to his argument. "Surely, it's very clear. The three of them steal a child. After the kidnapping they contact the parents. They force them to remain silent by threatening the welfare of the child. Then they asked for a ransom. The father, according to instructions received, reports to Little Lowee's bar and is sent on to the abandoned building where the kidnappers have found a temporary haven. He finds Colette. The negotiations go sour, there's an argument and . . ."

". . . the father kills Colette," completed Dijk.

Vledder looked at DeKok for confirmation.

"Exactly . . . yes. The father kills Colette. After the crime he panics and flees. Then Fred takes the child away from the Sisters and renews the contact with the parents. But this time the father is afraid to show himself again. After all, as far as he knows he may be wanted for murder. He sends his wife to visit Fred in the attic room at Harlem Street. The negotiations sour, there's an argu . . ."

"And the mother kills Fred," interrupted DeKok with a steel face.

Vledder looked at him evenly, pressed his lips together.

"Yes, the mother kills Fred," he asserted.

DeKok did not react. He rose from his chair and started to pace up and down the detective room. He stopped after a few times up and down the room and halted in front of the window, balancing on the balls of his feet. There were deep thought wrinkles in his forehead and his eyes were slightly narrowed as he looked out over the rooftops of the centuries old Quarter.

He had stood here many times. It seemed he had been involved with crime for ages. It had turned him gray and a network of wrinkles had developed around his eyes. How many murders had he investigated during his career? Thirty? Forty? A hundred? With a sudden shock he realized that he had lost track of the number. All those people, all those individuals, all those men and women he had cared about . . . he had forgotten how many of them there were. But they had all been important at one time or another. Especially after they had died. How strange, he reflected, they all took on a new importance after death, while most of them had been ignored while alive, he reflected without bitterness. He contemplated it with mild resignation, a calm acceptance of what he could not change, but would never stop trying to improve.

He turned away from the window and seated himself again behind his desk. Leaning on his elbows, he rested his head on top of his folded hands.

"If," he began carefully, "Vledder is right and the child has been stolen in order to get a ransom, then it's going to be difficult to find the parents. They don't have to come out in the open. Because the child, the cause of it all, is back where he belongs now that Fred has been killed. They can just sit back and let things develop." He turned toward Dijk. "Did you find the bar where Fred made his phone calls?"

"Yes," answered Dijk. "It was *The Blue Grape* on Inner Brewer Street."

"You're sure he called from there?'

"Yes."

"Where to?"

Dijk looked pained.

"It was no longer possible to find that out," he admitted regretfully. "Both calls were local calls. He used the phone behind the bar and paid for the calls."

"What time did he get to the bar?"

"Around eight. He left again around ten. He left with a girl."

Dijk nodded, unaware of the bombshell he was preparing.

"A good looking girl with long black hair. She wore an open blouse and a multi-colored skirt."

"Marianne," whispered Vledder.

16

DeKok's eyes narrowed.

"Marianne," he exclaimed, "Marianne was with Fred Mellenkamp?"

Dijk shrugged his shoulders resignedly.

"I've never seen Marianne, but if the description is accurate, it was Marianne."

"And they left together?"

"According to the barkeeper. They had been together all along, they shared a table in the back."

"Did they come in together?"

"No, the girl was there first."

"No mistake possible?"

"What about?"

"About Fred."

Dijk shook his head decisively.

"The barkeeper of *The Blue Grape* knew immediately who I meant. Fred used to come often. He even knew his first name."

"And Marianne?"

"The barkeeper had never seen her before," smiled Dijk. "He even contemplated asking her to leave."

"But why?"

"He thought she was a 'free-lancer', waiting to pick up a customer."

DeKok stared past the young Inspector. Momentarily he seemed uncertain about a course of action. Then he slapped a flat hand on the desk. It was as if he had decided. Suddenly he became very active. He stood up and stretched out a hand toward Dijk.

"You're going to attend the autopsy this afternoon," he ordered. "You show Dr. Rusteloos the piece of pipe we found. He can compare that with the wounds. But first get the official identification out of the way. Ask the neighbor if he wants to come along with the father . . . you better leave the mother at home," he advised. He paused a moment and then added: "And see what else you can find out about Fred's affairs with women."

Dijk nodded, signifying he had understood the instructions.

"But," he asked, "When the autopsy is done . . . what do you want me to do then?"

"Get in contact with the Commissaris and ask if the corpse can be released. Help the parents to arrange for the funeral."

"What else?"

DeKok went over to the coat rack.

"That'll keep you busy for a while, but if you finish early, wait for us to come back."

He grabbed his old, decrepit hat and his older raincoat. He motioned for Vledder to follow.

"Where are *we* going?" asked Vledder.

"To E-35," grinned DeKok.

"The Highway?"

"Very good," nodded DeKok, planting his hat firmly on top of his head and bunching the raincoat under one arm. "The Horst exit."

Vledder rushed to keep up.

"And then what?"

DeKok turned around.

"We're going to take a look," he said evenly. "We're going to take a look at the scene of a serious accident, last May."

* * *

They drove through the gray light of the early morning. There was hardly any traffic and DeKok tried to remember an old Dutch poem about slow, wide rivers through an endless lowland and ethereal poplars as silent guardians on the horizon. The poem often nagged at his mind and it irked him that he could never remember more than fragments, fleeting images. He also could not remember the poet. But at moments like this, when they left the city with a watery sun trying to penetrate the pervasive dampness, he was always reminded of it. The Dutch landscape is flatter than Kansas but always green. The green combined with the gray of the lifting fog and the shimmering of the waters to create an odd light, a light, thought DeKok smugly, that was typically Dutch and had been immortalized by hundreds of painters.

Vledder, as usual, was driving. There was a discontented look on his face. He could not fathom DeKok's intentions. Why he would want to drive in the direction of Zwolle, on the other side of the Zuyder Zee, and why did he insist on taking the long way around the inland sea. As had often happened before, he had the depressing feeling that he was outside the case, an onlooker, but not really a participant. It irritated him. The old man always listened with total interest to his theories and remarks, praised them voluminously at times, but in some strange, undefinable way, it always went different from the way Vledder planned, or expected. *That* irritated him most of all.

From time to time he glanced at DeKok who, also as usual, was sprawled in the passenger seat of the small car. The collar of his raincoat was pulled up high and his old, felt hat had been pulled deep over his eyes. Suddenly Vledder realized that he loved the old man, admired him. And for other reasons other than his undoubted qualities as a detective. Vledder suddenly realized that DeKok was the closest thing to a "good" human being he knew.

The pouting look disappeared from his face. He slowed down slightly, reducing the rattling noise of the car somewhat. With a wry grin he shut down the communications gear.

"What . . . eh, what sort of serious accident," he asked in a friendly tone of voice.

DeKok pushed himself up.

"A car accident."

"What does that have to do with the present case?"

DeKok waved nonchalantly.

"Everything . . . I hope." He pushed his hat back on his head and more or less flattened his collar. "Anything new about Marianne? I mean, her origins?"

Vledder shook his head sadly.

"Since Breda turned out to be a bust, I'm a bit at a loss where to look next. I already tried The Hague, the Central Registry. But they were no help." He paused, keeping his eyes on the road. "That car accident . . . surely there must be hundreds of serious accidents every day?"

DeKok smiled.

"And you want to know . . . why the Horst exit of E-35?"

"Yes."

DeKok turned toward his young friend.

"In early May Marianne, Colette and Bobby were hitchhiking near the clover-leaf, the intersection for Bilthoven. We'll pass that spot in a moment."

Vledder nodded.

"And they got a ride to Amsterdam."

"Exactly. Peter Vries, a friendly truck driver on his way back from Hanover, picked them up. On the way to Amsterdam a conversation of sorts developed. Marianne said at that time that the previous evening she had seen an accident with three dead." He sighed deeply. "Tragic, of course, but on the face of it no more than an idle remark, as far as *our* case is concerned."

Vledder threw him a sharp look.

"But you pursued it?"

DeKok nodded calmly.

"When there was no Marianne Vanburen known in Breda, I wondered if the *accident* could be a lead. You see, if there had been an accident near Breda, she *had* to be from there, she would have been there. Wherever the accident had happened, she was near it at the time."

"But how could you be sure of the date?" wondered Vledder.

"That was easy. I called the trucking company for which Peter Vries is driving. I also asked them on what date in May he returned from Hanover. It turned out to be the thirteenth."

"So, the accident must have happened on the twelfth," smiled Vledder.

"Yes," said DeKok easily. "There was only *one* accident involving three deaths on the twelfth. It happened near the Horst Exit of E-35."

They remained silent and entered the intersection near Bilthoven. Vledder slowed down some more. DeKok looked around. A bow of roads, he thought. Big, concrete ribbons, interlacing and intertwining. The thought of ribbons occupied him for some time. That's what girls used to wear in their hair when he was a boy. Big, colorful ribbons. Beautiful Lisa used to wear such a ribbon. She had been the girl next door and the best looking girl in school. DeKok smiled at the sweet memories of beautiful Lisa and their first, shy kisses behind the barn.

Vledder roughly tore the memories apart.

"When did you know?" he asked.

"What?" DeKok had been lost in thought.

"About the accident . . . near Horst."

DeKok rubbed the back of his neck.

"Yesterday," he said tiredly. "I called yesterday morning."

Vledder grinned.

"Then why, if you don't mind my asking, are we in such an all-fired hurry to get there all of a sudden?"

DeKok's expression changed.

"Last night," he began earnestly, "I suddenly realized how important that accident was."

"How . . . important?"

DeKok pushed his lower lip forward, organizing his thoughts.

"There were two things," he said calmly. "Two things in our case that suddenly seemed to jump at me. In the first place there was Fred Mellenkamp's arm. And then . . ."

"You mean the number that was written on his arm," interrupted Vledder.

"Yes, that number."

"One-two-five-nine-one," grinned Vledder, a bit bashful. "What could be the significance?"

DeKok took his notebook from his pocket and held it so that Vledder could see the number written there.

"If," he went on, "you were to place slashes between the numbers, what do you get?"

DeKok did just that and wrote "12/5/91".

Vledder glanced at the numbers.

"A date," he exclaimed, "twelve May 91, the date of the

accident."* He gave DeKok an admiring look. "Fantastic," he said out loud. "It wasn't a phone number at all, but a date, the date of the accident." He paused, concentrated on his driving. "But why?" he asked after a long silence. "Why did Fred write the date on his arm?"

DeKok smiled thinly.

"Because *he* hadn't seen the accident. He had not been a witness . . . he wasn't sure of the date."

Vledder could not help looking at his old partner. The VW almost crossed the center line as Vledder's attention was distracted.

"Marianne," he said hoarsely. "Marianne gave him the date and he wrote it on his arm."

Vledder recovered from his momentary lapse and they drove on in silence. DeKok allowed himself to sprawl back in the seat and Vledder contemplated new developments. When he saw the sign that announced the Horst Exit, he tapped DeKok on the arm and pointed. DeKok pushed himself again in a seating position.

At the end of the exit ramp, Vledder parked the car on the side and, a bit stiff, they emerged from the car. They looked around. To the right, at the bottom of the dike was a farm. The pale sun played across a long row of shiny milk cans next to the driveway. To the left they could just see the narrow strip of water now designated as *Veluwe Lake* and the huge dike that protected this part of Holland from what had once been the Zuyder Zee and had caused the smaller dike on which they found themselves to lose its primary function. It was still, presumably a back-up for the larger dike, but it was also used as a roadbed for E-35. All of it, the lake, the huge dike and the land beyond had all, at one time

---

* In Europe the day is written before the month. The same date in the U.S. would have been written as 5/12/91, i.e. May 12, instead of 12 May.

formed part of the sea on which DeKok's father had made a living as a fisherman.

"Is this the place?"

DeKok did not answer. He ambled away from the car and crossed the viaduct that spanned the highway. He stopped in the middle and looked down at the traffic. Traffic had increased, it roared away in both directions.

Vledder came to stand next to him.

"Do you know how the accident happened?"

"Not exactly, that is, I've no details. The car must have somehow gotten off the road and hit the overpass. I think that the driver missed the exit, noticed it and then lost control of the car. It has happened before, especially at high speeds." He turned half around, leaned against the parapet. "Just a little farther, in Ermelo, is a post of the State Police. They made the report. Ask if you can take a look at it. I'm very much interested to know who was involved in the accident."

"Aren't you coming?"

"Just go by yourself," said DeKok, shaking his head. "I'll wait here."

After the young Inspector had left, DeKok remained leaning against the parapet, deep in thought. The sun climbed higher and the morning chill disappeared. The traffic on the road below was now in full swing. Endless streams of vehicles roared by in both directions. DeKok wondered what the traffic had been like three months ago . . . just before midnight when the accident happened. Where had Marianne been at that time? Here? At the same spot where he stood now? He looked around. Where could she have come from at that hour . . . and where was she going?"

He knew about Ermelo. It was an extensive village with a predominantly Calvinistic population. There was an abundance of bucolic beauty, but it was not known as a haven for homeless people. Outsiders were limited to idyllic campgrounds, expensive vacation hotels and summer cottages. Now, in summer, it was busy and there were more tourists in the village than inhabitants. Some families transplanted their entire entourage from the city for the length of the summer, while the breadwinners continued to commute. But in the middle of May the season had hardly started. What did Marianne hope to find here? What was she doing here? How did she wind up here? Thinking, he left the viaduct and walked down the narrow road at the bottom of the Interstate.

A man on a bicycle left the farmyard he had noticed earlier.

A white bucket dangled from the handle bars and a dog, a drab colored beast of indeterminate lineage, jumped playfully after the bicycle. The man suddenly realized the dog was following. He stopped and leaned a wooden shoe on the road. The dog, wagging its tail, came nearer. The man shook his head decisively and stretched an arm out toward the farm.

"Back," he commanded, "back, Bobo."

The dog pulled its head between its shoulder blades and the tail drooped between its hind legs. Slowly it turned to go back to the farm house. The man watched for a second and then pushed his bicycle back into motion.

DeKok stood as if nailed to the ground. It was as if someone had suddenly penetrated his brain with a long needle.

"Bobo," he stammered, "Bobo."

It took a while before he was again able to move. As fast as he could he pursued the bicyclist, his arms waving. DeKok at speed was always a comical sight. Only some cows benefited from the spectacle.

* * *

The woman placed the enameled kettle on the kerosene stove and sat back, off to the side. Her hands in her lap. Farmer Hemminga pulled a large bowl of steaming coffee toward himself and heaped sugar into it. He stirred with total concentration.

"Marianne used to come here often," he said after a long silence, nodding in DeKok's direction. "She used to sit there, where you're sitting. In the same chair. She used to stay around for hours, especially in the evenings." He shook his head in wonderment. "Without saying much at all. Actually, she hardly ever said anything much. But you could see that she felt at home, here. Protected. That's why my wife and I never sent her away. Even when it was getting late." He smiled ruefully. "Usually we go to bed with the chickens and get up with them."

"And the child?"

"She always had him with her. A nice boy . . . a real friendly child." He pointed at the dog, that lay at his feet, softly snoring. "Bobo is a good watchdog and not at all friendly with strangers. When he's not chained up he chases everybody out of the yard, even the mail man." He smiled again. "Not that we get that much mail," he added thoughtfully. "But the child could do anything with the dog. It was a pleasure to watch. Sometimes they slept together in the basket." His wife looked non-committal.

"A wonderful child," the man continued with tenderness in his voice. "I've four kids of my own . . . all went to college . . . no interest in the farm." He pressed his calloused hands around the bowl and sipped carefully from the steaming liquid. "But as sweet and obedient as that little man, no, mine never were like that. Sometimes I used to tell Marianne: 'Leave him here, I'll make a farmer out of him'."

The gray sleuth rubbed his chin. Then he slurped unashamedly from his own coffee and looked at the man over the rim of his bowl.

"Did she react at all to that?"

Farmer Hemminga shook his head vehemently.

"Of course not. Not a chance. Marianne wouldn't even consider it. Whenever I mentioned it, she'd just leave . . . as if she thought I was serious . . . as if she were afraid I would really take the child away from her."

"She was afraid of that?"

"Yes, absolutely. That child was her life and it showed." He stared in his coffee. "Not at all what you'd expect from such a young girl," he mused.

"How do you mean?"

"Well, at that age . . . you'd expect them to be more geared for pleasure, dancing, whatnot. Such a beautiful, lively girl. But, nossir, every night she'd be here. After all, we're hardly her age group."

DeKok nodded his understanding.

"And when she left here . . . where did she go? Did she live around here?"

Farmer Hemminga shrugged his shoulders.

"She wasn't from around here. She didn't belong here. I think she came from some large city . . . ran away from home, most likely. She used to be vague about that."

DeKok leaned forward.

"But where did she live around here? She had to sleep somewhere, didn't she?"

Framer Hemminga calmly drained his bowl of coffee.

"I never asked. One day she came to ask for some milk. It was the beginning of March and pretty cold. She had a little bucket with her and carried the child on her arm. At first I thought she was a gypsy, they come around once in a while and I usually let them use one of the pastures. I thought it strange, because usually the gypsies ask permission to camp, before they come to the farm. They trade, you know. Anyway, my wife said at once that she couldn't be a gypsy, the child was too blond."

"Then what?"

"I chatted her up a bit, put some milk in her bucket and gave her some eggs. The next day she came again . . . with the child and the bucket." He paused, stared at his empty coffee bowl. "There are a number of summer cottages nearby. Nice little houses for those who like that sort of thing, with all the comforts of home, so to speak. They belong to people from town, you see. They're usually only occupied in the summer, vacation, or some such thing." He smiled and DeKok suddenly realized that this farmer had probably never taken a vacation. "Anyway," continued the man, "in winter and early spring they're usually just empty. I think that Marianne and her child lived in one of those cottages."

"With permission?"

Farmer Hemminga rubbed the back of his hand across his nose.

"She wasn't the type to ask permission," he smiled. The tolerance of the Dutch broke through the strict Calvinistic lifestyle of the farmer and his wife.

"Did you ever see her in company of a young woman, or a young man?"

"No," the farmer shook his head, "only with the child."

DeKok reached into his inner coat pocket an pulled forth the picture of Bobby.

Farmer Hemminga looked at the photo while his wife peered from the distance. The man nodded slowly.

"That's the child," he said, a bit absent-mindedly, "Yes, that's the child."

"You couldn't be making a mistake?"

The rugged face of the old farmer looked pained.

"Children's faces change so fast," he said. "But Marianne was here, day after day, for almost two months." He sighed. "She's been gone for almost three months now."

"She didn't say goodbye?"

Farmer Hemming bowed his head, rubbed his knees.

"No," he said sadly, "she never said goodbye." There was a tremble in his voice. "Suddenly she was gone. It hurt us a lot. We were good to her ... two months ... to her and the child. Not for a reward. Our motto is *do well and don't look back*. We didn't expect gratitude, the wife and I. But we had hoped that she trusted us enough to let us know where she went." He looked at DeKok with a tear in the corner of his eyes. "Isn't that so, sir?"

DeKok chewed his lower lip and nodded.

"She could have told you," he agreed. He studied the facial characteristics of the old farmer. It struck him that Marianne had been able to create feelings of love even in this stiff, tough farmer.

Mrs. Hemminga, who had hardly moved at all and had not spoken a word, now stood up. There was a barely suppressed agitation in her movements as she walked over to the enameled kettle. There was a hint of resentment in her voice as she lifted the kettle.

"I don't think she was a very *good* girl." Her voice sounded hard. It surprised DeKok. "She had a small child," the woman went on, "and didn't know the father. Whether you're from the town, or from the country ... that's ... that's not *decent*." She gestured, the kettle in one hand. "And if you ask me, she had something to do with that accident as well."

DeKok was astonished.

"What accident?"

She pointed outside.

"There, at the exit, near the viaduct. She disappeared the same night."

17

They drove back from Ermelo in the direction of Amsterdam. The speedometer hovered around 100 kilometers per hour. Vledder, of course, was again behind the wheel. His face was pale and his eyes were red-rimmed. He glanced at DeKok.

"Why were you at the farm?"

The gray sleuth yawned. A night without sleep affected him more than it used to do in the old days.

"Marianne used to visit there often," he said nonchalantly, "together with Bobby."

Vledder was taken aback.

"With Bobby?"

DeKok nodded resignedly.

"Since the beginning of March."

Vledder grinned without mirth.

"Bobby was around already ... I mean, it's *her* child."

"It looks that way."

The younger man was startled.

"But ... it's Marianne who insisted all long that the child was Colette's"

"To mislead us," said DeKok, pushing himself up in the cramped seat. "It's the only reason I can think of. But I suspected for some time that Marianne was the mother. You remember what happened when I told her that Colette had never been pregnant?"

"She fainted."

"It must have been a shock for her. She had no way of knowing that the autopsy could discover the fact. Most likely she never even considered an autopsy."

"But," gestured Vledder, "why?" His voice was full of emotion. "Why this masquerade? What was the use of saying that the child belonged to Colette?"

"Colette Maesen was dead," said DeKok wryly. "She could not testify. And with that we lost the last chance of discovering Bobby's parents. I'm sure that it was on her mind."

"I don't see it," said Vledder, irritated. "What's so important about the heritage of the child?"

DeKok pressed his lips together, a steely look in his eyes. Then he took a deep breath.

"Because of the heritage of the child, *two* murders have already been committed," he said grimly.

They drove on in silence. Soon the intersection near Bilthoven was again in sight. DeKok placed a hand lightly on Vledder's arm.

"Stop right here . . . careful."

The young Inspector brought the car to a stop on the shoulder. He pointed through the windshield.

"Hereabouts Marianne met Colette."

DeKok nodded slowly.

"And how far is it from here to the Horst exit?"

"About thirteen miles."

The older man stared into the distance.

"It was the middle of the night," he said pensively. "Between here and the Horst exit there are no places where you can hitch a ride."

Vledder looked confused.

"You think she walked that distance?"

"Yes. With a heavy backpack and Bobby on her arm."

"But why?"

"Because she fled . . . in a panic . . . away from the place where the accident happened."

Vledder lowered his head on the steering wheel. He was suddenly very tired. He rubbed his eyes.

"It was a terrible accident," he said softly. "I talked to the sergeant of the State Police who was first on the scene. The man still has nightmares. Apparently the car must have hit the supports of the viaduct at a high rate of speed and almost immediately burst into flames. It was an inferno. The sergeant was powerless to do anything. He had to watch the people in the car burn to death."

"Dreadful," said DeKok. It sounded like a prayer.

"They had to wait for the fire brigade," continued Vledder. "After they had arrived, all they could do was recover the charred remains."

"Do you have a copy of the report?"

"Here you go." Vledder reached backward and picked up a large envelope from the back seat.

"Is Marianne Vanburen listed as a witness?"

"No." Vledder shook his head. "There were no witnesses. The accident was reconstructed based on the available evidence. You were right. The general opinion is that the driver missed the exit, tried to correct for it and lost control. There was a long brake path, just past the exit ramp."

At what time was the accident reported?"

"Exactly seven minutes past midnight."

"How?"

"Emergency phone along the road."

"Was there any indication that the driver did indeed want to leave the highway at the exit?"

"Yes, they were on their way to a doctor."

"Who . . . they?"

"The victims. Husband and wife, Soren, and their child from Bilthoven. They had called a Doctor Grootkamp in Ermelo around half past eleven. The child had difficulty breathing and a high fever. They were worried and didn't want to face the night. Doctor Grootkamp advised them to come as quickly as possible."

"And the car at the viaduct belonged to the Sorens?"

"Yes, a blue Mercedes, license tag GN-9132."

"And the Soren couple and their child were in the car?"

"As far as the identification of the remains could determine," said Vledder sadly.

DeKok remained silent. He stared somberly through the windshield. After a long pause he spoke.

"I understand," he said softly. He gestured in the direction of the complicated intersection.

"Pick your way through it. We're going back."

"To the exit?"

"No, to Ermelo. I want to talk to Doctor Grootkamp."

Vledder covered his face with both hand.

"I'm tired. I want to sleep," he protested.

DeKok took a deep breath.

"So do I," he said unfeelingly. "There's a barber near the station in Ermelo. We'll have a shave." He looked at his young colleague. "It's the only concession I'll make."

Vledder started up and raced the engine.

"Slave-driver," he hissed between his teeth.

DeKok's reaction was lost in the noise of the engine.

* * *

Dr. Grootkamp's consulting room was cozy, a bit old-fashioned with a long settee, leather chairs and a roll-top desk near the window. A text was displayed on the wall: *A merry heart doeth good like a medicine, but a broken spirit drieth the bones.*

"Proverbs seventeen, verse twenty-two," smiled DeKok.

An older man, dressed in a rumpled white coat entered the room. DeKok turned around and stretched out his hand.

"Good morning, doctor," he said affably, "We're glad to find you in the office. If at all possible, we'd like to talk to you."

Dr. Grootkamp settled himself on the settee and gestured toward the easy chairs.

"Please sit down," he invited. He took off his glasses. "Inspectors from Amsterdam," he said with a creaky voice. "Perhaps I better take a good look at you." He pulled a handkerchief from his pocket and commenced to polish his glasses. He replaced the glasses with hands that shook slightly and looked carefully at Vledder and DeKok. There was a merry twinkle in his hazel eyes.

"Surely my fellow citizens haven't committed any crimes?"

DeKok gave him a tired smile.

"Where there's people, there's crime. Twenty centuries of Christendom haven't changed that."

Dr. Grootkamp shrugged his shoulders.

"What are a mere twenty centuries?" he said disparagingly. "Contemporaries of Einstein should know that." He looked at the gray sleuth. "Do you know anything about human nature?"

DeKok did not react. He was very familiar with the debating skills of the Calvinists and he did not feel like getting involved in a pointless conversation with the old doctor. He had himself been brought up as a Calvinist and he knew that those debates could be endless.

"On the twelfth of May," he began businesslike, "there was a serious accident near the Horst exit of E-35. A young couple and their seriously ill child were on their way to you. They perished in a horrible manner."

Dr. Grootkamp's face fell.

"It was tragic," he said softly. "I've been blaming myself ever since. Perhaps I should have gone to them, instead of them coming here. But I was tired that night and I had been in bed for less than fifteen minutes . . ."

"Please, you do not have to excuse yourself, doctor," interrupted DeKok. "But I wonder why they didn't take the child to a doctor in their hometown. There are doctors there, surely."

"Oh, yes," admitted the old doctor. "Eminently qualified physicians." He made a vague gesture. "But you know how that goes, it's a matter of trust. She . . . Mrs. Soren, was my patient since she was a child. I helped her into the world. I had, and still have, the entire Molenwick family as patients."

"Molenwick?" asked DeKok. He looked baffled.

"Lydia," smiled the doctor, ". . . Mrs. Soren," he clarified, "was born a Molenwick. She used to live here in Ermelo with her parents at Emma Lane . . . until she got married."

"And they still live there?"

"Who?"

"The parents."

"239 Emma Lane," confirmed the doctor. "The house is a little off the road." He looked at DeKok, suspicion in his eyes. "I don't . . . I don't know," he hesitated. "Why do the police have this sudden interest in an accident that happened months ago? Surely it was thoroughly investigated at the time? Young Soren was upset, he made a mistake."

DeKok nodded calmly.

"Indeed," he said. "That's the way it was ... just an accident." He paused. "But yet ... I would like to speak to old man Molenwick."

The doctor looked shocked.

"Why? I mean, is something the matter? Has he done something?"

DeKok ignored the questions. He placed both hands on his knees and came out of the chair. He looked down on the old doctor, observed the silver-gray hair.

"Do you understand human nature?" he asked without mockery.

Dr. Grootkamp rose as well.

"The Molenwicks are decent folks," he said vehemently. "The accident was quite a blow to them. Lydia was their only child. In one, unholy moment, they lost everything. Mrs. Molenwick is still very ill. She still hasn't been able to deal with the accident, with the loss." He raised a shaking hand. "I forbid you to visit them. It's medically not sound to rake it all up again."

DeKok turned around and without a word walked toward the wall. He passed the text with the golden letters and approached the window. He stopped in front of the old-fashioned desk. For just a moment he hesitated. Then he took a stuffed animal from the top of the desk.

"Dr. Grootkamp, whose koala is this?"

* * *

The quaint, old Station Street in Ermelo was busy. Women in colorful clothes and men in unaccustomed shorts walked up and down the street, going from store to store. Children whined for ice cream and soft drinks and thousands of bicycles mixed with the pedestrian traffic. DeKok stepped into a side street. The busy scene which he was able to enjoy so much in his beloved

Amsterdam, was an intrusion at the moment. It interfered with his thinking and pushed aside the thoughts of the murders.

Vledder walked beside him, a serious look on his young face.

"But it's possible," he said, not for the first time.

"What?"

"That Dr. Grootkamp keeps a stuffed koala in his office for his smaller patients."

"Sure," said DeKok tolerantly

"There's no reason why it should be Bobby's koala," persisted Vledder. "There must be thousands of those toys. Besides ... there's no resemblance at all between Dr. Grootkamp and the man described by Little Lowee. The doctor is much older. He's got to be at least sixty-five, seventy maybe."

"It takes too long," growled DeKok, "to ask all his patients how long he's kept a koala toy in his office."

"I liked him," said Vledder stubbornly. "We used to have a doctor just like that when I grew up."

DeKok wiped the sweat off his brow with a large, red handkerchief.

"He didn't want us to visit the Molenwicks," he said moodily. "And I bet he's on the phone right know, preparing them for our visit."

"What do you want?" laughed Vledder. "It's his right. He's protecting his patients."

"That old man must not interfere with my investigation," said DeKok sharply. "He'll get in trouble that way."

Vledder threw him an amazed look.

"You're being unreasonable. I can understand the doctor's attitude. Opening old wounds is never a healthy thing to do."

DeKok stopped suddenly, turned full toward his younger colleague and looked at him for a several long seconds. His face looked like a thundercloud just before it burst.

"Two people have died in Amsterdam," he said bitingly. "Do you remember that? Young people!" He shook his head, as if to clear it. "They didn't hit a viaduct. It was no *accident*. They were killed in cold blood."

* * *

Emma Lane, as was to be expected, was an upscale street with wide chestnuts and tall birches. Every town in Holland has a so-called "kings neighborhood" where the streets are named after members and former members of the Dutch Royal house. Emma had been the queenmother of Wilhelmina, Holland's first queen who governed in her own right. Wilhelmina, still much beloved, assumed the throne in 1898 and there have been no kings in Holland since. Generally the "kings neighborhood" in a Dutch town is where one finds the notables and the well-to-do citizens.

DeKok stopped at the corner of a narrow path. Two low, brick walls with heavily ornamented wrought iron lanterns indicated the entrance to number two hundred and thirty nine.

The gray sleuth pushed his hat further back on his head, pulled out his large, red, farmers handkerchief and wiped the sweat off his forehead.

"This is where it is," he said sluggishly.

Vledder pointed at the sanded path that wended its way to the large, manor-type house.

"Do we have permission to enter?" he joked.

DeKok put away his handkerchief and laughed.

"As long as we're not refused entry ..." He did not complete the sentence but stared into the distance. A well-built man came down the sandy path. He wore knickerbockers and a jacket of sturdy tweed. A big, black dog paced him at the end of a leash. DeKok studied the man, saw the ruddy face, the black, graying hair and took a step forward.

"Mr. Molenwick?" he asked.

The man was obviously annoyed.

"Yes," he snapped back.

DeKok lifted his hat in a polite gesture and showed his winningest smile.

"My name is DeKok . . . with, eh, with kay-oh-kay." He waved in the direction of Vledder. "And my colleague, Vledder. We are," he explained, "with the police in Amsterdam."

"Inspectors?"

DeKok agreed that it was so.

"We came to Ermelo in order to have a talk with you about the tragic accident that happened near the Horst exit, about three months ago."

Molenwick looked at the Inspector for a long time.

"I . . . I don't understand," he said hesitatingly, ". . . what I can add to that. The local police and the State Police have thoroughly investigated that already."

"That's exactly what the doctor said," observed DeKok. He did not add anything to the cryptic remark, but seemed to be absorbed in the observation of a nearby sparrow. Molenwick did not answer for several seconds.

"The old doctor?" he asked, finally.

"Dr. Grootkamp," smiled DeKok. "We just left him. A very pleasant man, much concerned about the welfare of his patients. He told us your daughter was involved in the accident."

Molenwick's face hardened. The ruddy outdoors look disappeared.

"And my son-in-law," he said harshly. "And my grandchild. They found . . . they died together. You understand . . . it's painful for me to speak about it." He stopped talking and shook his head with emphasis. "I refuse to discuss it any further." He pulled brusquely at the leash, turned around and walked away.

DeKok followed him. The dog growled, lifted its head and pulled back its upper lip, revealing a long row of large, healthy teeth. DeKok was not impressed. He had found that dogs seldom attacked him. And this time, too, the dog subsided and allowed DeKok to walk along beside its master.

"I cannot accept your refusal," said DeKok, a bit sharp. "If you don't want to talk to me, I'll have to contact your wife. Perhaps she'll be more cooperative."

Molenwick stopped suddenly and turned toward the old Inspector. There was a dangerous light in his brown eyes, almost malevolent.

"You leave her alone, you hear?" He spoke angrily, hard, with a definite threat in his voice. "You leave my wife out of it."

"Is that still possible?"

Molenwick was baffled. He looked at DeKok. His expression was a mixture of surprise and suspicion.

"You better explain what you mean by that," he blustered, but there was uncertainty in his tone of voice.

DeKok shrugged his shoulders, as if it were a minor point.

"Can she stay out of it? Just how much is she involved? How much does she know about this entire affair?"

Molenwick burst forth with a short, barking, joyless laugh. The dog moved restlessly.

"Affair . . . affair," he mocked. "What kind of affair." He paused. Then he changed his manner. "My dear man," he said condescendingly, "if you want to know about this accident, then why don't you go to the police. Ask for the files, or whatever you people call it. No doubt you'll find the answers to all your questions."

DeKok smiled darkly.

"Everything, Mr. Molenwick? Will I read in the reports that a few days ago you were in Amsterdam to pick up a child?"

The man's mouth opened. His jaw dropped. The dog's leash slipped out of his hand.

"I . . . eh . . ." He shook his head in bewilderment, without conviction. "I was never in Amsterdam."

DeKok's smile became wider. He cocked his head at the large, heavy man.

"Would you like me to confront you with my good friend, Little Lowee? Do you really want me to drag him away from his prosperous establishment in order to make a formal identification?" There was sweet sarcasm in his voice. "Or," he continued, "would you like to renew your acquaintance with Old Karl, who still fondly remembers you every time he has a drink from your hundred guilders?"

Molenwick pressed his lips together. His fleshy face was pale, his nostrils quivered. But for all that he looked determined.

"There must be a mistake. I . . . I don't know what you're talking about."

It was a feeble defense.

DeKok pointed at the house.

"Let's go inside," he proposed. "We can discuss this intelligently and in private."

Molenwick shook his head stubbornly.

"I have nothing to say to you."

DeKok studied the man. His sharp gaze traveled over the stubborn features. He read fear in the brown eyes. Fear and uncertainty. The corners of the mouth trembled and yet the face was sympathetic. The round cheeks and the full lips gave evidence of an openhearted happiness, a joviality, that did not fit in with the type of crime he suspected. The old cop took a deep breath.

"Mr. Molenwick," he began patiently, "it's useless to deny you were in Amsterdam. I know you were there and I can prove it. I also know that you were approached about a child . . . a sweet blond boy and that you received his picture. I also think I understand why you responded to the approach." He paused for effect. "But what I *don't* understand, Mr. Molenwick, is why you killed Colette Maesen."

18

"Not me . . . not me . . . not me," Molenwick repeated over and over again, as if in a daze. He waved his arms in the air and was obviously losing control of himself. The dog whined, barked and jumped nervously up and down.

DeKok was a bit at a loss. He spoke soothingly to Molenwick and tried to calm him down. But to no avail. The man was getting more and more out of hand. For a moment DeKok contemplated shaking him, perhaps slapping him, but the dog might misunderstand that. He was in no mood to deal with an upset man and an upset animal at the same time.

"Not me . . . not me . . . not me," repeated Molenwick at the top of his voice. His voice was getting hoarse and his eyes rolled wildly. A woman approached from the direction of the house, there was fear in her attitude and her hair streamed behind her. She took hold of the man.

At almost the same time a black Cadillac stopped at the beginning of the driveway. The broad tires squealed on the asphalt and the old doctor emerged from the car. In passing, he gave the cops a devastating look.

"I told you to stay away," he hissed.

DeKok did not answer. Resignedly he watched how the woman and the old doctor led Molenwick away. The dog jumped ahead of them, barking less, but still whining from time to time as it looked back at the trio.

A man in an impeccable blue suit came out of the car, from the back seat. He held a briefcase under his left arm and he approached DeKok with an arrogant stride, his head slightly aloof.

"Dr. Grootkamp alerted me. My name is Kraal, I'm an attorney."

"And?"

The man swallowed.

"I . . . eh, I look after the interests of Mr. Molenwick."

DeKok looked slowly, almost insolently from the neat crease in the pants to the closed jacket with the subdued tie. He then studied the face for several seconds. He did not like the face.

"You're his mouthpiece?"

The man became red.

"Your behavior is outside the bounds of all decency," he bristled. "I will file a complaint against you. Your superiors will hear about this."

DeKok nodded slowly.

"Very well," he said amiably. "My name is DeKok . . . with kay-oh-kay. Please be sure to spell my name correctly."

* * *

DeKok was silent as he stared out the windows of the VW. The landscape passed him by in broken, half-seen images. He was thinking about the various conversations and impressions of the last few hours . . . Farmer Hemminga . . . his wife . . . the old doctor . . . scared Mr. Molenwick . . . the arrogant lawyer. The last thing he worried about was a complaint. There were new viewpoints, hints. He weighed those as much more important than the next reprimand from the Commissaris. He rubbed his chin in a pensive movement. In spite of all the new insights, he had the feeling he was still a long way from the solution. He moved in his seat. A cold chill ran along his back. He was cold, tired and hungry. The beneficial effect of the shave they had allowed themselves had long since dissipated. He stole a glance at Vledder behind the wheel, noticed the gray streaks in the pale face.

"As soon as we're in Amsterdam," said DeKok cheerfully, "we'll go to *Kembang Java* in the Damrak. We'll have a complete *rijsttafel*. We've earned it. Then we'll get a few hours sleep."

"A few hours?" yawned Vledder. "I feel like I could sleep for days."

"We can't afford too much sleep," said DeKok seriously. "The sooner we solve this case, the better. If Molenwick gets the chance to organize his judicial defence forces, we won't have a chance any more. He's a rich man with a lot of influence."

"Since when did that make a difference to you?" asked Vledder.

"Never," answered DeKok tranquilly. "But it doesn't hurt to keep it in mind. If for no other reason than to nullify the effect on the course of justice."

"So you're convinced he killed Colette?"

DeKok shrugged his shoulders.

"There's no question that he's the man who was identified by Lowee. He's the one who received directions for the abandoned building in Emperor Street. The description fits . . . a bit dignified, about forty-five, gray at the temples. Just to be sure, we'll double check it tonight."

"Tonight?"

"Yes."

"How?"

DeKok smiled slyly.

"For a while Mr. Molenwick was an Under-secretary for the Treasury Department. I'm sure his picture is on file with a number of newspapers and magazines. Perhaps even together with his wife."

Vledder smirked.

"We show the picture to Lowee and Old Karl and..."

Nodding, DeKok interrupted.

"We'll show the picture of Mrs. Molenwick to Aunt Marie."

"The boarding house keeper in Harlem Street?"

"The very same."

Vledder looked wide-eyed.

"You ... you really think she's the last person to have visited Fred Mellenkamp?"

DeKok rubbed the corners of his eyes.

"I wouldn't be surprised," he said tonelessly. "It's within the nature of things to be expected."

Vledder moved in his seat, sat up straighter behind the wheel. Some color had come back in his cheeks. He was all fired up again and full of enthusiasm.

"But then she's the one who killed him," he exclaimed. "As I suggested." He swallowed, rubbed his suddenly dry lips with the back of his hand. "Then ... then *she* is the one who has the child."

* * *

DeKok spread the pictures out before him. His friend, Bram Brakel, a reporter, had been delighted to help out. The pictures showed Mr. Molenwick in several poses during official functions. His wife, too, was in some of the pictures. She smiled happily at the camera.

The gray sleuth looked up from the pictures and directed his gaze at Robert Antoine Dijk. This time the young Inspector wore a distinguished blue suit with a pearly gray necktie. The combination was appreciated by DeKok's conservative nature.

"How was the autopsy?"

"Nothing special," answered Dijk, shrugging his shoulders, a bit bored. "Fred Mellenkamp was indeed killed with a piece of gas pipe. There was no doubt about it, according to Dr. Rusteloos."

"Has the body been released?"

"Yes, permission for burial is in your desk drawer. This afternoon, together with the father, I arranged for the funeral."

"Had an opportunity to talk about affairs with women?"

The young man pushed the photographs aside and leaned confidentially on the desk.

"Among many others," he said mysteriously, "there was a certain Marianne Vanbugger."

DeKok sniffed.

"A Marianne . . . what?"

"Vanbugger," laughed Dijk. "It doesn't sound very appetizing. Marianne thought the same. That's why she insisted on being called Vanburen."

"No wonder we couldn't find her in any Registry at all," snorted Vledder.

DeKok looked at Dijk.

"Go on," he urged.

Dijk consulted his notebook.

"Marianne Vanbugger was born in Breda and was an orphan at the age of nine. Father and mother died shortly after each other. Then followed a sorrowful trail from one orphanage to another until, on her fifteenth birthday, she was taken in as a foster child by a family Mellenkamp."

DeKok rubbed his skull, ruffling his gray hair.

"So, that's how she knew Fred."

"And how," grinned Dijk. "They had an affair almost from the day she entered the Mellenkamp household. When Fred's parents finally discovered what was going on, they sent her away."

"When was that?"

"About two and a half years ago."

"And Bobby?"

Dijk made a sad movement with his hand.

"Old man Mellenkamp knew nothing about a child." He moved his chair and sat closer to the desk. "And you want to know something ... there's no record of the child's birth anywhere."

"Nowhere?"

The young Inspector shook his head decisively.

"I checked everything. Officially Marianne Vanbugger is *not* the mother of a child. Of course, that doesn't mean that she couldn't *have* a child. There are a number of cases when the birth of a child is simply not reported. Gypsies especially have a tendency to forget the formalities. Usually we find out when they contact Social Services for the child allowance."

DeKok's eyes narrowed as he looked at Vledder.

"But Fred knew," he said. "Remember, when we were talking to Squinting Rika and Rika objected to having trouble with the authorities? Fred assured her that wouldn't be a problem with *that* child. As I recall, her exact words were: *Then the guy opened his mouth and said it wouldn't happen with that child. I just couldn't deduct him from the taxes, or expect a child's allowance.*"

Vledder smiled. He could look it up, but he had no doubt that DeKok had just quoted Rika verbatim. Suddenly the young man caught his breath.

"But," he said breathlessly, "that means that Fred could be the father of the child."

DeKok pushed his lower lip forward, pulled on it and let it plop back. He repeated the annoying gesture several times.

"I'm beginning to get a glimmer," he said at last, "why Fred was killed."

Slowly he rose and pushed the pictures into a heap and then into an envelope.

"Come on," he said, "we're going to see Little Lowee."

"Me too?" asked Dijk.

"It's about time you two get to know each other," nodded DeKok.

As they walked out of the detective room, the phone on DeKok's desk started to ring. Vledder walked back to answer it. After a few seconds he covered the mouthpiece and beckoned urgently to DeKok.

"A Mrs. Molenwick is downstairs," he whispered when DeKok had retraced his steps. "She's asking for you."

DeKok hesitated for just a moment. Then he pushed the envelope with pictures into Dijk's hands.

"Go by yourself," he said hastily. "As soon as you have a positive identification, you come right back here." Then he turned to Vledder. "Tell them to let her come up."

* * *

DeKok leaned both elbows on his desk. From above folded hands he gave her a long, observing look. He estimated her to be in her early forties. A handsome woman, he realized. Much more beautiful that the picture he had in his mind of her running, fear on her face, hair streaming out behind her. Her eyes were a disturbing, phosphorescent light green, craftily accentuated by a subdued makeup. Her mouth was wide and sensual with a nervous, hesitating smile. She crossed her slender legs and clutched her purse in both hands on her lap.

"Did your husband send you?" There was just a hint of mockery in his tone. "Or are you here on the advice of your attorney, the no doubt able Mr. Kraal?"

She looked at him evenly, disregarding the mocking tone.

"I'm not the sort of woman who can be sent."

DeKok made an expansive gesture.

"So you're here on your own accord? Excellent, really excellent."

"And of my own free will," she said earnestly. "I should have done so days ago. That became clear to me this afternoon."

"After my visit to Ermelo?"

"I hardly noticed you this afternoon," she smiled wanly. "I only noticed how my husband reacted. He's not strong enough to withstand such tensions."

"Nevertheless, he'll have to account for the murder of Colette Maesen."

She shook her head calmly, patiently.

"My husband didn't kill that girl. I realize that the circumstances are against him, but he didn't do it. He would not have been able to do it." She fell silent, took a deep breath. "Really, its all my fault. I'm rather independent and don't like to rely on other people . . . especially not in a case like this." She looked at him and there was a hint of fear in the green eyes. "I had not foreseen these murders, Mr. DeKok. And I don't understand why they happened."

DeKok leaned toward her, holding her eyes in his gaze.

"When did you get the letter?"

"What letter?" she asked with a catch in her voice.

"I presumed," answered DeKok tiredly, "that there was a letter . . ."

She lowered her head.

"Lydia was our only child. We were very happy when little Richard was born. Especially my husband. He was besotted with the child. We would have liked to have a son of our own, but..." She stopped abruptly, took a firmer grip on her purse. "You can imagine what the accident meant to us. In one blow life had lost all purpose for us. It was as if a hole had been drilled through our souls ... creating an empty spot, never to be filled. It was almost unbearable in the beginning." She swallowed and suppressed the tears in her eyes. "Then ... three months later, we received a letter. At first you don't want to believe it, you understand? You keep telling yourself ... it isn't true ... it's impossible. But the letter was so real ... so convincing."

"Do you still have the letter?"

With shaking hands she opened her purse and took an envelope out of it.

"I should have brought it at least a week ago," she said softly. "But ... under the circumstances ... you don't think in terms of police."

DeKok looked at both sides of the envelope, took the letter out of it and read aloud:

Dear family Molenwick,

You do not know me. My name is Colette Maesen. About two years ago I had a child, a boy. I called him Bobby, just because I liked the name. I am not rich and was not brought up in a sheltered and protected environment like your daughter. Yet I loved my Bobby as much as she loved her child.

They call me names. They call me a hippie, a wanderer, a gypsy, an addict. The last is true. I do use what are called 'controlled substances' and therefore I probably do not fit into polite society. I have moved around a lot and have often been chased away.

Early this year there was an empty summer cottage in Ermelo and I went to live there with Bobby. Those were the happiest months of my life. Bobby became sick in May. I was afraid to go to a doctor, because they might take away my child. I nursed him as much as possible, but one morning he died. It took me a long time to decide what to do and I decided to bury him myself. I had brought him into the world by myself and I would escort him out by myself. I stole a spade from a farmer's yard and during the night I walked, the shovel over my shoulder and Bobby under my arm, toward the little beach at the lake, near Horst. Before I even reached the viaduct, I heard the screaming of brakes, followed by an enormous crash. I went to look. A car had hit one of the pillars at full speed. A man and a woman were sitting in front. They were dead. I could see that at once. But a child was seated in the back seat, still strapped in a child's seat. He was just about the same size as my Bobby. There was nothing the matter with him. He was just crying.

Perhaps you will curse me for what I did next. But I do not regret it. I took the child out of the car seat and put my Bobby in his place. I also took some clothes and a little koala bear.

The smell of gasoline became stronger. I think the tank leaked. Because I wanted to make sure that my crime, the exchange of the children, would not be discovered, I lit the gasoline with a candle that had been meant for Bobby's funeral. The car burned immediately. I looked from a distance until the first people arrived. Then I went away.

DeKok became silent and placed the letter on his desk. The silence around DeKok's desk became suffocating. The normal noises of the large detective room seemed to be muffled by thick layers of cotton wool. DeKok looked up and encountered the astounded look of Vledder. Then he looked at the woman.

"I can understand," he said softly, "how you would take the letter seriously. It's indeed very convincing."

Mrs. Molenwick reacted unexpectedly. She stood up and slapped a flat hand on the desk.

"But it's true," she cried out loud. "Every word is true. My husband has seen the child himself."

"When?"

"That day," she swung her purse violently through the air. "That day in the abandoned building at Emperor Street." She resumed her seat, calmer. "If you read on," she said, "you'll find the instructions and a threat not to speak with anyone about it. I can remember the words as if they're branded in my brain: *I went to bury a child once. It will not be difficult to do it again.*" She shook her head. "I don't know how many times I've repeated those words to myself."

"Your husband followed the instructions?"

"Yes, with a picture of little Richard he went to that bar. The barkeeper sent him on to Emperor Street. There he met a young woman who said she was Colette Maesen and had written the letter."

"There was nobody else?"

"No."

"What did she look like?"

"Small, blonde, skinny."

DeKok nodded to himself.

"Please go on."

"First of all, of course, we wanted to be *sure*. My husband and I had agreed on that beforehand. We wanted to be absolutely sure that Richard was still alive. If we could be convinced on that point, we were prepared to do *anything* to get the child back."

"Even murder?"

She looked at DeKok, a defiant look on her face.

"Even murder," she said without blinking.

"Colette Maesen showed the child to your husband?"

"She took him out of a closet," she said with a broken voice. "My husband was immediately convinced. He recognized his grandchild at once. The blond hair . . . the clothes. There was no doubt. My husband wanted to take the little boy with him, then and there, but Colette didn't allow that. My husband was in despair. Give me the child, he said, I will get you the money. I promise. I'll come and bring it myself. That sort of thing."

"How much did she want?"

"Half a million . . . in cash."

"And you knew that?"

"No," she answered, shaking her head. "There was no mention of an amount in the letter. But we understood full well that Colette wanted a ransom. Of course, my husband didn't carry that kind of cash around and that wasn't the intent of the meeting, anyway. The meeting was meant to be informative only."

"And you wanted to be sure yourself, as well?"

"Exactly. My husband only had a few thousand in his wallet. He offered her that, as a kind of down-payment."

"But Colette wouldn't budge?"

"No," she said softly, staring into the distance. "No, he couldn't change her mind. He was only allowed to take the little koala with him. To help convince me."

"And?"

She lowered her head. This time she could not suppress the tears. They dripped on her hands and on the purse in her lap.

"It was Richard's little koala. He had pulled an ear off at one time. I sewed it on myself."

DeKok let her be. He did not rush her. When he thought she had recovered a bit, he went on.

"What sort of agreement did you make?" he asked gently.

She replaced the little pink handkerchief, which she had used to wipe her tears, into her purse.

"My husband asked for three days in order to raise the cash. Colette agreed. The agreement was that my husband would be back at the same address in three days."

"With the money?"

"I blamed my husband bitterly," she admitted. "I told him that he had handled it all wrong. He shouldn't have left, just like that. He should have just taken Richard away from that slut. But my husband is too much of a gentleman. He would never have been able to do such a thing. That's why it's absurd to think he could have killed anyone, especially a woman."

DeKok ignored the last remark.

"Three days later you went back with him ... with the dog?"

"Indeed," she glanced at him briefly. "We took Max with us ... as protection ... for me, my husband ... a lot of money."

"I see," nodded DeKok. "And when you came to the abandoned building, there was nobody there?"

"Empty ... not a soul. My husband was beside himself. He had been busy night and day to get the money together. And then my constant accusations ... it must have been hell for him." She opened her purse and again took out the pink handkerchief. "We asked around ... carefully ... and then we heard that a girl had been killed in the building."

"You didn't know?"

"Of course not. We had lived in a daze for three days ... certainly didn't look at newspapers. After our visit to the empty building, we bought some papers at the railroad station. We looked through them on the way back and found the report about the abandoned building and the murdered girl. We knew at once that it was Colette Maesen. It couldn't be anybody else. Everything checked ... the place ... the age ... the initials CM*

... but not a word about a child. We couldn't understand it. We were devastated when we drove back to Ermelo."

She fell silent. The handkerchief had now been reduced to a small ball of material, but her lips were compressed in a determined expression.

DeKok rubbed the bridge of his nose with a little finger.

"But surely," he said matter-of-factly, "that wasn't the end of the day."

"What do you mean," she frowned.

DeKok gave her a pleasant smile.

"That same evening you received a phone call ... around ten o'clock. A male voice informed you that he had little Richard and that you could deal with him concerning the ransom. New hope sprang up, but you wanted to be sure. Again. You asked the man a hundred questions ... about the child ... about the accident ... if the man knew where it happened. The man left the phone booth for a few seconds and came almost right back with the correct date: May 12, 1991. You were convinced and arranged a meeting."

She looked at him with disbelief. Unperturbed, DeKok went on.

"The next morning you went to Amsterdam, to Harlem Street. Your husband had made a mess of it, the last time. This time you would handle it yourself. You were determined ... no matter what ... to return home with the child. The man you were to meet was a murderer. You were convinced of that. He was the man who had killed Colette in order to gain possession of the child ... and the ransom."

---

* In the Netherlands, the full names of crime victims and suspects of crimes are never printed in the media. In many cases the full names are not published, even *after* a trial. People are identified by initials and the place of birth, i.e. "The police today arrested CM of Amsterdam." Complete records are, of course, available from the courts. The policy is instituted to protect the privacy of victims, those that are merely accused, but later found innocent as well as the (often innocent) family members of criminals.

Vledder watched fascinated as methodically and without seeming to be aware of what she was doing, she tore the little handkerchief into tiny pieces.

"You weren't taking any chance," continued DeKok. "As soon as the landlady had told you where to find him, you climbed the stairs. You listened, felt the doorknob and discovered the room wasn't locked. You went inside. The man was on the bed, next to the child. Praying to God he wouldn't wake, you crept closer and hit him on the head with . . ."

"No, no, no," she screamed suddenly, covering her face in her hands. "He was dead . . . he was already dead."

19

Vledder handed her a glass of water. She took it with shaking hands. The edge of the glass rattled against her teeth as she drank. DeKok watched, outwardly unmoved, with a granite face. Vledder took the empty glass back. She gave him a grateful look and Vledder returned an encouraging smile. She dropped the shreds of her handkerchief on the floor without noticing it, produced another small handkerchief from her purse and delicately dried the corners of her mouth. She adjusted her blouse.

"He was dead," she repeated in a shaky voice. "He was dead on the floor and there was blood on his face and head."

"And the child?"

She shook her head.

"He wasn't there. Little Richard was gone. He *had* been there. I saw milk and rusks and jam."

"Then what?"

"I walked away, softly." She made a helpless gesture. "I descended the stairs and left. My husband was waiting outside in the car. I told him what had happened and he panicked. He said they would suspect me of the murder and he worried that the license tag might already have been noticed. We rushed back to

Ermelo, at wit's end. We didn't know what to do and we finally decided to call our doctor."

"Dr. Grootkamp?"

"Yes. We told him everything . . . the letter . . . Colette and the dead man in Harlem Street. He advised us to wait. The murderer was ultimately interested in the money. Somebody was bound to contact us."

"And?"

"We didn't hear a thing." She shook her head sadly. "Now I'm so afraid that they have harmed him . . . that we'll never see him again." She placed a hand on his arm and looked at him with big, begging eyes. "Can't you help us, Mr. DeKok? Can you give us back our little Richard? It's worth anything we have."

"I'm paid by the City of Amsterdam," growled DeKok.

She shook her head vehemently.

"I don't mean it that way. I don't want to bribe you, or anything. But you know people. You know who they are . . . what they think . . . what they do. *You* could negotiate with them."

DeKok stood up. Her hand fell off his arm.

"I don't negotiate," he said moodily. "I don't negotiate with anybody." He looked down at her. His harsh demeanor softened. "Go back home, to Ermelo," he said gently. "As soon as we know something, I'll contact you."

She rose from her chair, a nervous smile on her face.

"I . . . I can go?" There was amazement in her voice. DeKok pursed his lips and nodded.

"If your husband is waiting for you downstairs," he said cynically, "give him my regards and remind him that hospitality is an old Dutch custom."

She blushed deeply, shook hands with the gray cop and walked out of the room. Both Inspectors watched her go. Then Vledder snorted.

"Rich people always think they can do everything with money." He snorted again. "And then, when things go wrong . . ."

DeKok stared at the closed door.

"A desperate woman," he said pensively. He glanced at Vledder. "You know," he said, "sometimes rich people are just poor people with money."

The telephone on DeKok's desk rang. Vledder walked over and lifted the receiver. He listened and held it up towards DeKok.

"For you."

"Who?"

"Robert Antoine."

DeKok took the receiver.

"Very good . . . so it checked out . . . Little Lowee positively identified Mr. Molenwick and Aunt Marie confirmed that Mrs. Molenwick was the woman who asked after Fred Mellenkamp. That makes it . . ." He stopped in mid-sentence. "What!?" His face changed. "Stay where you are," he ordered curtly, "we're coming."

He beckoned to Vledder as he walked over to pick up his hat.

"They spotted Marianne," he explained.

* * *

There was quite an uproar in the half-dark, intimate establishment of Little Lowee. The place was fuller than normal. Whores were grouped at the various tables and spoke loudly in offended tones. Josie the Aussie hung at the bar and her dark eyes spat fire.

"It was her," she exclaimed with conviction. She waved in the direction of the diminutive barkeeper. "I told you right-a-way: That crazy sheila is back again."

Lowee nodded agreement.

"Squinting Rika saw her as well. Yesterday afternoon . . . with the child."

DeKok's eyes narrowed.

"With the child?"

"She carried him on her arm."

"Why didn't you call at once?" asked DeKok, censure in his voice. "You knew I wanted to know."

Lowee shrugged his shoulders.

"Well," he said unwillingly, "I figure you'll come to have a drink soon enough and I could of tole you then."

Josie pulled at DeKok's sleeve.

"I can tell you where she is."

"Where?" asked DeKok, turning toward her.

"In one of those empty warehouses at Anthony Cross Street, the big one."

"How do you know?"

"When I saw her tonight," she smiled cunningly, "I sent Little Willy after her. Go and see where she goes, I said."

"And who," asked DeKok, "Is Little Willy?"

"A new girl," answered Josie. "Just started a few weeks ago. She has a window at Aunt Gert's. She can show you exactly."

"Never mind," said DeKok. "I know the place you mean." He motioned to Dijk and Vledder and left the bar. Outside he stopped and pointed at Robert Antoine.

"Go get a car and meet us at Anthony Cross Street. Drive via Dam, Dam Street, Old Street and High Street and then wait at the corner. Make sure the car has a spotlight that works."

Dijk nodded and ran away in the direction of the station.

Vledder and DeKok walked in the opposite direction and soon reached the corner of Anthony Cross Street via Cleavers Canal.

It was dark and deserted. There were no occupied residences left in the street. A few warehouses were also waiting for the wrecking ball. DeKok glanced up at the facades. Most of the windows were dark and without glass. An occasional candle flame flickered here and there, indicating occupation by some homeless person, or a tramp.

Vledder slowed down.

"It's a warren in there," he said. "All those old buildings have been connected simply by knocking holes in walls. You can pass through and over the buildings all the way to Crooked Tree Ditch. I was talking to a guy from Narcotics. They recently did a raid here."

"So," observed DeKok, "there's no telling where she will exit?"

"Exactly."

DeKok nodded to himself.

"But," he said mildly, "I'm not about to call out the troops in order to intercept a girl and a child."

They crossed the street and DeKok flashed his light into a portico without door. The lobby was filled with debris and trash. Carefully he stepped inside.

"Watch out," he cautioned. "There's no bannister on the stairs."

Vledder followed. Warily they climbed the stairs, keeping their balance by keeping in touch with the wall. On the second floor they stopped and pushed open a door. The lights of the flashlights roamed the room. A young man was sleeping on a stack of flattened cardboard boxes. DeKok came closer and tried to shake him awake. The young man did not react. DeKok pushed the dirty hair out of the face and opened an eyelid. The eye did not react to the light.

"Stoned," he commented somberly.

They left the room and climbed the next set of stairs. From an open door there came a yellow light. They entered and found a girl on the edge of a filthy mattress. DeKok didn't think she was older than fifteen. A candle burned in front of her and illuminated a packet of smoking tobacco and a loaf of bread. Not until the shoes of the men entered the weak circle of light made by the candle, did she look up. There was no surprise, or shock in her eyes. After a single glance she lowered her head and continued to roll a cigarette.

DeKok found matches in his pocket, hunkered down and offered her a light. She licked the cigarette paper and ignored the proffered flame, leaned forward toward the candle and lit the homemade cigarette that way. Unemotionally DeKok blew out the match that was threatening to burn his fingers.

"Have you seen a girl with a child?" he asked in a friendly tone of voice.

She looked at him with total incomprehension.

He repeated the question in English.

A smile fled across the young-old face.

"A young girl ... a baby." She pointed at the ceiling. "Upstairs," she added.

DeKok slowly unwound himself from the uncomfortable position.

"Thanks," he said simply, "thanks a lot."

They left the girl with her candle and walked up to the fourth floor. Everything was pitch dark. They listened intently but there was no sound. Carefully they opened a door and peered inside. The room was empty. In a corner was the door of a closet, closed off by a slanted piece of wood. Vledder played his flashlight over it.

"Would she ... again?" he whispered.

With shaking hands he removed the plank and opened the closet door. At the bottom of the closet, in an old cardboard box stuffed with rags, they found the child. He waved both arms in the air and made kirring sounds as he tried to catch the beam of the flashlight.

DeKok lifted the child out of the box.

"Bobby." His voice was hoarse. "Poor kid." He pressed the child against his chest and laid his cheek against the pale face. Then he handed the child to Vledder.

"Take him away."

"And you?" asked Vledder as he accepted the child.

"I'll wait for her to come back."

* * *

He sat in the dark, his broad back against the closet door and waited patiently. Next to him was the board that had locked the closet and on top of that was his flashlight. He had left instructions with Dijk to honk the horn three times when he saw anybody enter the building. But so far everything had remained silent. He wondered why it had taken so long, why he had not seen it sooner. Somewhere he must have made a mistake. But where? Had she disarmed him? Had he been too lenient because she was a woman, a young woman to whom he had been strangely attracted, almost from the start?

In the middle of his musing he suddenly became fully alert. Outside a car horn had sounded three times. He took the flashlight in his hand and struggled upright. Soundlessly he moved toward the landing and listened. Somebody was coming up the stairs. A light step ... the shuffling of feet, barely perceptible. He went back into the room. He stopped next to the door opening and pressed himself against the wall. Tensely he waited for her to come in.

Suddenly she was there. A soft air current seemed to pass him by. He could not see her, but he knew her exact location. He could hear her breathing. The footsteps went to the left, to the closet door. He knew her hands were groping for a plank that was no longer there. He heard her breathing quicken and understood her fear.

He stepped aside and blocked the door opening. Then he flipped on his flashlight and aimed the beam in the direction of the sound. There she was, as he had expected ... leaning forward, groping into the closet.

He directed the light toward his own face.

"It's me, Marianne ... DeKok ... I've come to get you ... you know why."

She straightened out and approached him slowly. Her head was bowed so that the long hair hid her face. Suddenly, in an unexpected release of power and strength, she knocked the flashlight out of his hand. The light did not go off, but it rolled over the floor. DeKok gripped her shoulder. She fought, twisted, struggled like a cornered rat. DeKok tried to get a better grip on her and encircled her wrist. Suddenly she bit him in the ball of his hand. The involuntary reaction caused him to lose his grip.

She fled, toward the landing, down the stairs. DeKok picked up his flashlight and followed her as quickly as possible. He could hear her hasty footsteps on the stairs. Suddenly there was a scream, followed by a dull thud and then silence.

Momentarily DeKok froze in position. He realized what had happened. Balancing himself against the wall, he descended the stairs.

He found her at the bottom, on the granite floor of the lobby. Her long legs were uncovered to above the knees and the black hair fanned out around her head. Her face was pale and her eyes were closed.

DeKok knelt down next to her. The tips of his fingers found her neck, searched for a pulse. He noticed the small movements of her lips. He leaned forward and brought his ear close to her mouth.

"Bobby," she whispered, "my Bobby."

A wave of pity seemed to overpower him. It started in his chest and threatened to choke him. His eyes burned and he felt tears he was unable to suppress. He swallowed, tried to rid himself of the lump in his throat. Without success. His tears dropped on the bloodless lips.

Suddenly he sensed someone behind him.

He looked up and saw the concerned face of Robert Antoine Dijk. He looked one more time at Marianne, then straightened out her skirt to cover her legs and rose with difficulty.

"Call the paramedics," he said shakily.

He turned and waddled away, into the dark street.

20

With his bandaged right hand, DeKok opened his front door and welcomed Vledder. The young man laughed shyly and brandished a large bouquet of roses.

"How . . . eh, how is it?"

DeKok lifted the bandaged hand.

"Bitten . . . by a cat."

Vledder laughed and came in.

"Robert Antoine here already?"

"Yes," nodded DeKok, "he's with my wife and talking up a storm."

"The braggart," snorted Vledder, "what sort of suit is he wearing this time?"

"Who knows," laughed DeKok, "Heavenly blue, or old rose. Maybe soft green. I don't know anymore, they all have the colors of ice cream."

They entered the living room. Mrs. DeKok rose and walked toward Vledder with outstretched hands. She received the roses with delight. She waved toward some comfortable chairs.

"Sit down," she invited cheerfully. "My husband was wondering what had happened to you."

The young Inspector looked somber.

"She's dead. I just heard the news as I was leaving the station."

"I know," nodded DeKok. "I visited her."

"When?"

"Last night. They came to get me. She asked for me."

"Did you speak with her?"

"Yes."

"Long?"

"Long enough."

"Were you there," asked Vledder tensely, "when . . .?"

"Yes." The gray sleuth bit his lower lip and turned aside. "I was there," he said softly after a brief pause. "It was very peaceful . . . very calm and peaceful. Much more peaceful than I expected." He wiped his eyes with the back of a hand. "She filled in the missing pieces for me and then she went . . . peacefully. Perhaps it was better that way. Her spine was broken in several places and there was other damage. She would never again have been able to walk . . . to dance."

A silence fell over the room. They stood together, motionless, in silent contemplation. DeKok glanced at the old-fashioned grandfather clock in the corner. Quarter past nine . . . more than fifteen hours since Marianne had died.

Vledder finally broke the silence.

"Strange," he said, "I thought she was a strange girl . . . definitely not normal. But I haven't been able to keep her out of my mind all day."

The older man placed his hand on the shoulder of his colleague.

"That's good," he said encouragingly. "That's very good. You should always keep your fellow human beings in mind. Think positive thoughts . . . the only way to understand people."

Mrs. DeKok intervened.

"Let's not get maudlin," she said briskly. "Please sit down. We have all night."

They sat down and DeKok lifted a venerable bottle of cognac from the small table next to his chair. He filled the waiting snifters and passed out the glasses.

"*Proost*," he said, a little too loudly, "to crime."

The younger cops looked at him strangely. They did not echo the toast. Vledder took a hasty sip and moved closer to the edge of his chair.

"Is the child gone?"

DeKok put down his glass.

"I took him to Ermelo myself, this afternoon," he said.

"To the Molenwicks?"

DeKok stared into the distance, a tender smile lit up his face.

"You know," he said slowly, softly, "that I found it difficult to say goodbye to the little man? I kept finding excuses to delay my departure. I just couldn't find the strength to leave Ermelo. I must have asked them a hundred times to take good care of the child. I made a proper fool of myself." He picked up his glass and slowly rocked it in his hand. "But then," he added, "I've seldom felt so close to a case."

Vledder looked at him with a certain amount of suspicion in his eyes.

"Was that because of the child?" he asked.

"Maybe," shrugged DeKok. "I don't know. Maybe because of the child and maybe . . . also because of Marianne."

Vledder swallowed, almost choked.

"What! Marianne?" he exclaimed incredulously. "you felt *close* to her? Involved? As far as I know, she killed *two* people."

"You're right," nodded DeKok.

"But why?" asked Vledder. "What was the purpose? Did she want all the money for herself?"

DeKok did not answer at once. He crossed his legs and nestled himself firmly in his easy chair.

"You're familiar," he said patiently, "with the letter that was sent to the Molenwicks. I've read it so often in the meantime, that, not unlike Mrs. Molenwick, I practically know the text by heart."

He suddenly sat up straight, gestured violently.

"Marianne," he said forcefully, *"knew nothing about the sending of that letter!"*

Vledder and Dijk reacted in unison.

"What!?" they said, clearly astonished. Dijk leaned closer.

"But . . . all those details in the letter . . . she was the only one who could know."

DeKok lowered his head and rubbed the corners of his eyes in a tired gesture. The sleepless nights were exacting their toll. He was very tired.

"Marianne," he said, less vigorously, but just as emphatically. "Had nothing to do with the blackmail, the attempts at extortion. It was Fred Mellenkamp's plan, the man who had studied law. He composed the letter and Colette Maesen was his submissive tool."

The gray sleuth looked up and met the eyes of his wife and the tense faces of the two young men. He hoped he could convince them.

"Marianne," he said in a normal tone of voice, "Had told the other two about the car accident. The accident had made a deep impression on her and she could not stop talking about it. Colette's health was failing rapidly. She needed more and more heroin and that costs. After Marianne met her near Bilthoven, Marianne felt responsible for the girl. She stole for her and helped raise the money for her addiction as much as possible. Fred had advised Marianne several times to get rid of her son. There were plenty of whores, according to Fred, who wouldn't mind paying for such a handsome little boy. Marianne played along, but in reality she was playing for time."

Vledder interrupted.

"Why prostitutes?" he asked. "Contrary to popular belief, they're not exactly in the higher income brackets. I mean, why did they wait until after the accident to offer the child to the Molenwicks?"

"Because they didn't know about the connection ... the connection between the rich Molenwicks and the child. You must understand ... Marianne had no idea about the identity of the people involved in the accident. Why should she read newspapers. She had not even bothered to inquire after the victims. She had no idea about the type of car and even less about the license number. It was no more than pure coincidence that Mellenkamp found out about the connection."

"How?"

"Because of a magazine article. The last few weeks before she died, Colette hardly ever left her mattress any more. Fred and Marianne drifted together. One day he and Marianne were having coffee in a bar near Gelder Quay and Fred idly flipped through some magazines. In one of them he came across an article about traffic safety. The accident near Horst was described by way of illustration, including all the piquant details about Mrs. Soren being the daughter of the former Under-Secretary of the Treasury Molenwick."

"Aha," grinned Vledder, "and that set the wheels in Fred's criminal brain to turning."

DeKok nodded.

"From Marianne's reluctance he had become convinced that his scheme of selling her child to a prostitute would never see fruition. Therefore he by-passed Marianne altogether and developed a more intimate relationship with Colette. He promised her all the heroin she could use and Colette agreed to negotiate with Molenwick."

Meanwhile all had managed to empty their glasses and Mrs. DeKok reached over, took the bottle and refilled the empty snifters.

"One afternoon," DeKok continued after a grateful glance at his wife, "the two conspirators made sure that Marianne was gone and Colette dressed the child in the clothes that Marianne had recovered from the accident. With the little koala in his tiny hands, she showed the child to Molenwick. We know from Mrs. Molenwick that he was immediately convinced and was prepared to pay the ransom." DeKok paused, sipped from his cognac. It seemed to steady him. "Then Colette made a mistake that would cost her her life."

"What mistake?" asked Robert Antoine Dijk .

"She forgot to take the clothes off the child."

"Why was that important?"

"Marianne *never* used those clothes. She didn't want her child to wear them. From Peter Vries, the truck driver, we know she allowed the child to be cold, rather than dress him in the good clothes she had in her bag."

"Why?" asked Mrs. DeKok.

"Let me tell it in my own way . . . Anyway, when Marianne came back from her shopping trip, she found the child all dressed up in his good clothes. She was surprised, because Colette never paid any attention to the baby. Suspicious, she asked for an explanation. Colette evaded her questions but Marianne was persistent and Colette finally confessed. She told her about Fred's plan and that a man had been to look at the child. Marianne was furious, felt betrayed. Betrayed by the woman she had taken under her wing, had cared for, had stolen for. There was an angry quarrel and when Colette said she was going to go through with the plan, that she would meet Molenwick again,

Marianne lost her temper, picked up a piece of pipe and bashed Colette over the head."

"The first murder."

DeKok took a sip from his drink.

"If you want to call it murder," he said thoughtfully. He took another sip. "I'd call it manslaughter," he added.

"A technicality, surely," objected Vledder.

"Maybe. But it wasn't premeditated. In any case, when Marianne discovered that Colette was dead, she was beside herself. It took a while before she could again think rationally and she soon realized that she couldn't hide the body for ever. After two days she thought she had found a solution."

"She came to us," grinned Vledder, "and asked for a grave. When we discovered the child, she said he belonged to Colette and that they had been blackmailing a man."

"A man," smiled DeKok, "who had taken the koala and was responsible for Colette's death." He scratched behind his ear. "I think we went wrong when we learned from Little Lowee that there was indeed a man who had inquired about a girl and a blond baby."

"She had thoroughly confused you both," observed Mrs. DeKok. Vledder thought he detected a slight smirk in her tone of voice, but decided hastily that he must have been mistaken.

"Yes, she fooled us," admitted DeKok. "From the very beginning I had the feeling that she was highly intelligent, despite her odd behavior at times."

Robert Antoine wanted to know more.

"And what about the second killing? The murder of Fred Mellenkamp?" he urged.

"That's rather simple to explain. Because Marianne had told us that the child was Colette's she could, of course, not prevent us from placing the little boy with the Sisters. But she watched him carefully and tried to get in contact with the child.

She followed Sister Angelica when she took Bobby to Wester Park and that is also how she saw Fred take the baby."

"She saw that?" asked Vledder.

"Yes. And of course she knew immediately why he wanted the child . . . he was going to try for the ransom on his own. She followed him and eventually she saw him go into the boarding house at Harlem Street. She watched for an opportunity to take the child back, but there was a long wait and she decided to wait in a nearby bar."

"*The Blue Grape*," smiled Dijk.

"Around eight o'clock," continued DeKok, ignoring the interruption, "she saw Fred come out of the building. She wanted to follow him, when she suddenly realized that he was heading straight for the bar. She changed her tactics and when Fred entered the bar, she was nice as can be. She told him that she killed Colette, but that it was a mistake and for half a million she'd be happy to relinquish her child. Fred is completely taken in. He tells her he has the child and all obstacles have been removed. It's now merely a matter of the exchange. Around ten he calls Molenwick and gets the wife on the phone. She dearly wants the child back and asks all sorts of questions. Fred is not aware of all the details, but with Marianne's help he's able to convince Mrs. Molenwick."

"The date," remarked Vledder. Mrs. DeKok immediately asked what he meant. While DeKok poured another round, Vledder explained about the date on Fred's arm. The significance of which they had almost missed, thinking it a phone number.

"After the phone call," resumed DeKok, "Fred takes Marianne home to his room and Marianne is reunited with her boy. When Fred is asleep, she slips out and finds a similar piece of pipe which had earlier served her so well . . ."

DeKok remained silent. He drained his glass and stared into the distance. The faces of the two young men were serious. They thought over what they had heard. They looked for gaps, incomplete information, things they wanted to ask.

Mrs. DeKok looked at her husband. There was a thoughtful look in her eyes. Her husband looked drained, tired, older than she had seen him for some time. She stood up and went to the kitchen and returned with several platters, heaped with delicacies.

Then she went back in the kitchen and soon the delicious smell of fresh coffee wafted through the house. When she returned to the living room for the second time, the discussion had become more general. Robert Antoine Dijk praised Mrs. DeKok's culinary efforts while he stuffed himself unashamedly.

DeKok remained quiet. He leaned back and listened to the bantering between his wife and the two young men. Carefully he stretched his legs and nursed his drink. After a while he joined again in the general conversation and treated his guests to a series of anecdotes from his early days on the force.

Soon, too soon, thought DeKok, it was late and the two young men took their leave. He accompanied them to the front door and wished them a cheery good night.

* * *

When he returned to the living room, he poured himself one more glass and nestled himself comfortably in his chair. With a sigh, he stretched his legs and accepted a cup of coffee from his wife. His wife sat down on the arm of his chair and hugged him. It surprised him. He looked at her with a question in his eyes.

"I always knew it was Marianne's child," she said calmly, with conviction. "I've known since you came back from Ermelo."

"I don't understand what you're talking about," he said weakly."

She smiled indulgently.

"That little boy wasn't Richard Soren ... he isn't the Molenwick's grandchild at all."

"They're convinced," he said evenly, avoiding her eyes.

"Who?"

"Mr. and Mrs. Molenwick are convinced he's their grandson. The arrogant, but able Mr. Kraal has already completed the paperwork to nullify the death certificate that was issued erroneously. Our report will facilitate approval and there'll be no doubt at all. I saw the pictures this afternoon and the resemblance is uncanny."

"But he's Marianne's son," persisted Mrs. DeKok.

"Of course," admitted DeKok resignedly. "There never was an exchange of children. It was something made up by Fred Mellenkamp. I'm sure that when he read the magazine article and saw the pictures, the resemblance between Richard Soren and his Bobby must have struck him."

"His Bobby."

"Yes. He was the father. When his parents sent their foster child away, Marianne was already pregnant. And Fred knew it and didn't lift a finger. Marianne was too proud to say anything. It was pure coincidence that, almost three years later, they ran into each other again."

Mrs. DeKok nodded her understanding.

"Fred Mellenkamp is dead," she said quietly. "He's beyond human judgement." She looked at her husband. "But what really happened the night of the accident?"

DeKok stroked her arm.

"Marianne was a restless young woman. When Bobby was asleep, she used to walk on the beach near Horst and dance on the sand. She saw the accident happen and went to see if she could help. The man and the woman were both dead on the front seat and little Richard, together with his clothes and the koala had been thrown out of the car. The child was still alive. She picked him up and carefully put him on the back seat. Then she turned to pick up the koala and the spread out clothing. While she did that, the car suddenly caught fire. It was quickly so hot and intense that she was unable to reach the car. She saw the child burn in front of her eyes."

Mrs. DeKok closed her eyes and shuddered.

"Marianne was horrified, to say the least. Her only thought was to get as far away as possible from the scene of the accident. She ran to the summer house, picked up Bobby and disappeared." DeKok looked at his wife. "Now you know why she never wanted Bobby to wear the clothes."

There was a long silence. Mrs. DeKok left the arm of her husband's chair and sat down across from him.

"Did you promise Marianne that you would take Bobby to Ermelo?"

"No." He shook his head sadly. "I promised her that I would make certain he would be well looked after."

"Is that why you took him to Ermelo?"

He stood up, paced up and down the room a few times. He stopped near the mantel piece.

"I thought hard about," he said finally. "There wasn't much time. Just a few hours to decide the fate of a child." He stuck out his chin. "I don't believe that rich children are necessarily happier than poor children. The balance sheet of the Molenwicks didn't enter into it . . . just their conviction, their conviction that Bobby was their grandchild. I also believed that I acted in Marianne's spirit. Marianne had never been happy in orphanages and foster homes. There was no other alternative. There was no third possibility." He looked at his wife. "What do you think?" he asked humbly. "Did I do wrong?"

She walked towards him. She took him by the arm and squeezed it against her. There was a proud and tender look in her eyes.

"You did very well," she assured him.

DeKok rubbed his face with his free hand and sighed a deep sigh. It sounded like a sigh of relief. Suddenly his face fell. He looked at her intently. He searched the features he knew so well.

"But how," he asked, "did you know?" There was a tone of wonder in his voice. "Everybody concerned is dead. Nobody else has a clue. Nobody could have given you a hint."

"A hint about what?" she asked innocently.

"That Bobby was Marianne's child and not the child . . . the Molenwick grandchild. Vledder and Dijk know now, of course, but they won't say a thing. The Commissaris accepted the report as written. Everybody else thought it perfectly normal that I took the child to Ermelo."

She nodded calmly.

"They were all convinced that the children had been exchanged after the accident."

"But not you?"

She shook her head. There was a secretive smile around her lips.

"Bobo," she whispered. "You remember? The word that Sister Angelica told you?"

DeKok narrowed his eyes. Suddenly the association came back to him.

"Bobo," he said, shocked. "Farmer Hemminga's dog."

She nodded at him, as if he had just solved a difficult puzzle.

"You see . . . it had to be Marianne's child. The Molenwick grandchild had never slept in the basket with the dog."

DeKok walked over to his easy chair and sank down in it, a look of devastation on his face.

"Bobo," he repeated to himself. "Of course! It completely slipped my mind. I should have known sooner. Bobo ... moments of intimacy and safety ... locked away in a child's mind ... Marianne's child."

"Never mind," soothed his wife. "In the end you *did* tie up all the loose ends."

About the Author:

Albert Cornelis Baantjer (BAANTJER) first appeared on the American literary scene in September, 1992 with "DeKok and Murder on the Menu". He was a member of the Amsterdam Municipal Police force for more than 38 years and for more than 25 years he worked Homicide out of the ancient police station at 48 Warmoes Street, on the edge of Amsterdam's Red Light District. The average tenure of an officer in "the busiest police station of Europe" is about five years. Baantjer stayed until his retirement.

His appeal in the United States has been instantaneous and praise for his work has been universal. "If there could be another Maigret-like police detective, he might well be Detective-Inspector DeKok of the Amsterdam police," according to *Bruce Cassiday* of the International Association of Crime Writers. "It's easy to understand the appeal of Amsterdam police detective DeKok," writes *Charles Solomon* of the Los Angeles Times. Baantjer has been described as "a Dutch Conan Doyle" (Publishers Weekly) and has been called "a new major voice in crime fiction in America" (*Ray B. Browne*, CLUES: A Journal of Detection).

Perhaps part of the appeal is because much of Baantjer's fiction is based on real-life (or death) situations encountered during his long police career. He writes with the authority of an expert and with the compassion of a person who has seen too much suffering. He's been there.

The critics and the public have been quick to appreciate the charm and the allure of Baantjer's work. Seven "DeKok's" have been used by the (Dutch) Reader's Digest in their series of condensed books (called "Best Books" in Holland). In his native Holland, with a population of less than 15 million people, Baantjer has sold more than 4 million books and according to the Netherlands Library Information Service, a Baantjer/DeKok is checked out of a library more than 700,000 times per year.

A sampling of American reviews suggests that Baantjer may become as popular in English as he is already in Dutch.

WHAT OTHERS SAY ABOUT BAANTJER AND HIS BOOKS

About BAANTJER, the author of the "DeKok" books: The Reader's Digest has already used seven books by Baantjer in *Het Beste Boek* (Best Books), to great enjoyment of our readers (*L.C.P. Rogmans,* **Editor-in-Chief, [Dutch] Reader's Digest**); A Baantjer book is checked out of a library more than 700,000 times per year (**Netherlands Library Information Service**); We have to put the second printing of his books on press before the first printing has even reached the bookstores, no matter how many we print (*Wim Hazeu,* **Baantjer's Dutch Publisher**); The style reminds me a bit of Georges Simenon. Fast, clever and satisfying (*Lucinda May,* **Mysteries by Mail**).

MURDER IN AMSTERDAM, the two very first "DeKok" stories for the first time in a single volume, containing *DeKok and the Sunday Strangler* and *DeKok and the Corpse on Christmas Eve.* (ISBN 1-881164-00-4): If there could be another Maigret-like police detective, he might well be Detective-Inspector DeKok of the Amsterdam police. Similarities to Simenon abound in any critical judgement of Baantjer's work (*Bruce Cassiday,* **International Association of Crime Writers**); The two novellas make an irresistible case for the popularity of the Dutch author. DeKok's maverick personality certainly makes him a compassionate judge of other outsiders and an astute analyst of antisocial behavior (*Marilyn Stasio,* **The New York Times Book Review**); Both stories are very easy to take (**Kirkus Reviews**); Inspector DeKok is part Columbo, part Clouseau, part genius, and part imp. Baantjer has managed to create a figure hapless and honorable, bozoesque and brilliant, but most importantly, a body for whom the reader finds compassion (*Steven Rosen,* **West Coast Review of Books**); Readers of this book will understand why the author is so popular in Holland. His DeKok is a complex, fascinating individual (*Ray Browne,* **CLUES: A Journal of Detection**); This first translation of Baantjer's work into English supports the mystery writer's reputation in his native Holland as a Dutch Conan Doyle. His knowledge of esoterica rivals that of Holmes, but Baantjer wisely uses such trivia infrequently, his main interests clearly being detective work, characterization and moral complexity (**Publishers Weekly**).

DEKOK AND THE SOMBER NUDE (ISBN 1-881164-01-2): It's easy to understand the appeal of Amsterdam police detective DeKok; he hides his intelligence behind a phlegmatic demeanor, like an old dog that lazes by the fireplace and only shows his teeth when the house is threatened (***Charles Solomon*, Los Angeles Times**); A complete success. Like most of Baantjer's stories, this one is convoluted and complex (**CLUES: A Journal of Detection**); Baantjer's laconic, rapid-fire storytelling has spun out a surprisingly complex web of mysteries (**Kirkus Reviews**).

DEKOK AND THE DEAD HARLEQUIN (ISBN 1-881164-04-7): Baantjer's latest mystery finds his hero in fine form. As in Baantjer's earlier works, the issue of moral ambiguity once again plays heavily as DeKok ultimately solves the crimes (**Publishers Weekly**); Real clarity and a lot of emotional flexibility (**Scott Meredith Literary Agency**); DeKok has sympathy for the human plight and expresses it eloquently. (***Dr. R.B. Browne*, Bowling Green State University**).

DEKOK AND THE SORROWING TOMCAT (ISBN 1-881164-05-5): The pages turn easily and DeKok's offbeat personality keeps readers interested (**Publishers Weekly**); Baantjer is at his very best. There's no better way to spend a hot or a cold day than with this man who radiates pleasure, adventure and overall enjoyment. A ***** (five stars) rating for this author and this book (**CLUES: A Journal of Detection**).

DEKOK AND THE DISILLUSIONED CORPSE (ISBN 1-881164-06-3): Baantjer has provided a fine and profound series of books (***Ray B. Browne*, Popular Press**); Baantjer seduces mystery lovers. "Corpse" titillates with its unique and intriguing twists on a familiar theme (***Rapport*, The West Coast Review of Books**).

DEKOK AND THE CAREFUL KILLER (ISBN 1-881164-07-1): DeKok is ever interesting, a genuine "character". More descriptive, however, is the compassion in DeKok's heart (**CLUES: A Journal of Detection**); This is entertaining reading (**Rapport**).

DEKOK AND THE ROMANTIC MURDER (ISBN 1-881164-08-X): A clever falsesuspicion story. Everyone should read these stories (**CLUES: A Journal of Detection**); For those of you already familiar with this loveable old curmudgeon, you're sure to enjoy this installment. Score one for the Dutch (***Dorothy Sinclair*, The Crime Channel**).

DEKOK AND THE DYING STROLLER (ISBN 1-881164-09-8): An intriguing story about youth and violence (**CLUES: A Journal of Detection**).

DEKOK AND THE CORPSE AT THE CHURCH WALL (ISBN 1-881164-10-1): Detective-Inspector DeKok returns in another solid offering from Baantjer (**Publishers Weekly**); Has enough red herrings to keep the most sophisticated expert guessing (**Rapport**); DeKok is a careful, compassionate policeman in the tradition of Maigret; crime fans will enjoy this book (**Library Journal**).

DEKOK AND THE NAKED LADY (ISBN 1-881164-12-8): This is the twelfth book about DeKok and his assistant, Vledder. This time it also means an even dozen murders. Baantjer spins his usual entertaining yarn (**Publishers Weekly**).

DEKOK AND MURDER ON THE MENU (ISBN 1-881164-31-4): One of the most successful achievements. DeKok has an excellent sense of humor and grim irony (**CLUES: A Journal of Detection**); Terrific on-duty scenes and dialogue, realistic detective work and the allure of Netherlands locations (**The Book Reader**).

TENERIFE!
by Elsinck

Madrid 1989. The body of a man is found in a derelict hotel room. The body is suspended, by means of chains, from hooks in the ceiling. A gag protrudes from the mouth. He has been tortured to death. Even hardened police officers turn away, nauseated. And this won't be the only murder. Quickly the reader becomes aware of the identity of the perpetrator, but the police are faced with a complete mystery. What are the motives? It looks like revenge, but what do the victims have in common? Why does the perpetrator prefer black leather cuffs, blindfolds and whips? The hunt for the assassin leads the police to seldom frequented places in Spain and Amsterdam, including the little known world of the S&M clubs in Amsterdam's Red Light District. In this spine-tingling thriller the reader follows the hunters, as well as the hunted and Elsinck succeeds in creating near unendurable suspense.

First American edition of this European Best-Seller.

ISBN 1 881164 51 9

From critical reviews of **Tenerife!**:

A swiftly paced, hard-hitting story. Not for the squeamish. But nevertheless, a compelling read, written in the short take technique of a hard-sell TV commercial with whole scenes viewed in one- and two-second shots, and no pauses to catch the breath (*Bruce Cassiday*, **International Association of Crime Writers**); A fascinating work combining suspense and the study of a troubled mind to tell a story that compels the reader to continue reading (*Mac Rutherford*, **Lucky Books**); This first effort by Elsinck gives testimony to the popularity of his subsequent books. This contemporary thriller pulls no punches. A nail-biter, full of European suspense (**The Book Reader**); ... A wonderful plot, well written—Strong first effort—Promising debut—A successful first effort. A find!—A well written book, holds promise for the future of this author—A first effort to make dreams come true—A jewel of a thriller!—An excellent book, gripping, suspenseful and extremely well written ... (**A sampling of Dutch press reviews**).

MURDER BY FAX
by Elsinck

Elsinck's second effort consists entirely of a series of Fax copies. An important businessman receives a fax from an organization calling itself "The Radical People's Front for Africa". It demands a contribution of $5 million to aid the struggle of the black population in South Africa. The reader follows the alleged motives and criminal goals of the so-called organization via a series of approximately 200 fax messages between various companies, police departments and other persons. All communication is by Fax and it will lead, eventually, to kidnapping and murder. Because of the unique structure, the book's tension is maintained from the first to the last fax. After his successful first book, *Tenerife!*, Elsinck now builds an engrossing and frightening picture of the uses and mis-uses of modern communication methods.

First American edition of this European Best-Seller.

ISBN 1 881164 52 7

From critical reviews of **Murder By Fax**:

Elsinck has created a technical tour-de-force. This high-tech version of the epistolary novel succeeds as the faxed messages quickly prove capable of providing plot, clues and characterization (**Publishers Weekly**); This novel by Dutch author Elsinck is so interestingly written it might be read for its creative style alone. It is sharp and concise and one easily becomes involved enough to read it in one sitting. MURDER BY FAX cannot help but have its American readers fall under the spell of this highly original author (*Paulette Kozick*, **West Coast Review of Books**); This clever and breezy thriller is a fun exercise. The crafty Dutch author peppers his fictional fax copies with clues and red herrings that make you wonder who's behind the scheme. Elsinck's spirit of inventiveness keeps you guessing up to the satisfying end (*Timothy Hunter*, **[Cleveland] Plain Dealer**); The use of modern technology is nothing new, but Dutch writer Elsinck takes it one step further (*Peter Handel*, **San Francisco Chronicle**); . . . Riveting—Sustains tension and is totally believable—An original idea, well executed—Unorthodox—Engrossing and frightening—Well conceived, written and executed—Elsinck sustains his reputation as a major new writer of thrillers . . . (**A sampling of Dutch press reviews**).

CONFESSION OF A HIRED KILLER
by Elsinck

A dead man is found in a small house on the remote Greek island of Serifos. His sole legacy consists of an incomplete letter, still in the typewriter. An intensive investigation reveals that the man may well be an independent, hired killer. His "clients" apparently included the Mafia and the Cosa Nostra. The trail leads from the Mediterranean to Berkeley, California and with quick scene changes and a riveting style, Elsinck succeeds again in creating a high tempo and sustained tension. A carefully documented thriller which exposes the merciless methods of organized crime. In 1990 Elsinck burst on the scene with the much talked-about *Tenerife!* which was followed, in 1991, with *Murder by Fax*. His latest offering has all the elements of another best-seller.

First American edition of this European Best-Seller.

ISBN 1 881164 53 5

From critical reviews of **Confession of a Hired Killer**:

Elsinck saves a nice surprise, despite its wild farrago of murder and assorted intrigue (**Kirkus Reviews**); Elsinck remains a valuable asset to the thriller genre. He is original, writes in a lively style and researches his material with painstaking care (**de Volkskrant, Amsterdam**).